MY NEAR-DEATH ADVENTURES

I ALMOST DIED. AGAIN.

ALISON DeCAMP

CROWN BOOKS
FOR YOUNG READERS
NEW YORK

Text copyright © 2016 by Alison DeCamp
Jacket art copyright © 2016 by Scott Nash

All rights reserved. Published in the United States by Crown Books for
Young Readers, an imprint of Random House Children's Books, a division of
Penguin Random House LLC, New York.

Crown and the colophon are registered trademarks of Penguin Random House LLC.

Visit us on the Web! randomhousekids.com

Educators and librarians, for a variety of teaching tools,
visit us at RHTeachersLibrarians.com

Library of Congress Cataloging-in-Publication Data is available upon request.
ISBN 978-0-385-39048-4 (trade) — ISBN 978-0-385-39049-1 (lib. bdg.) —
ISBN 978-0-385-39050-7 (ebook)

Printed in the United States of America
10 9 8 7 6 5 4 3 2 1
First Edition

To Sam.
Who always makes sure we're good.

CHAPTER 1

What now, Stan? Huh? What do you want to do now?"
Cuddy Carlisle's questions come at me like two hundred hungry mosquitoes buzzing around my head—they're hard to ignore and for some reason make me itchy.

"Do you have a rash?" Cuddy's eyebrows scrunch together as he peers up at me. "'Cause Mother says I am sensitive to rashes, Stan. I need to be careful."

I shake my head to reassure him. "No, no rash, Cuddy." Although just the mention of rashes and my skin starts tingling.

"Whew! That was a close one, wasn't it, Stan?" Cuddy chuckles before thankfully switching the topic. "Can we go to your house? Can I see that scrapbook of yours? Remember? You promised!"

It's true. I did. He was with me when I got the mail the other day. In it was a package from my good friend Stinky Pete.

He's a lumberjack, not a pirate.

Anyway, Stinky Pete sent me what is now my Most Prized Possession. My very own Mark Twain Self-Pasting Scrapbook. It's so fancy, it doesn't even need paste! Unfortunately, I told Cuddy he could see my scrapbook someday, and now I haven't heard the end of it. In fact, I haven't heard the end of a lot of things, like all three verses of "After the Ball," plus the verse that goes:

After the ball was over,
    Bonnie took out her glass eye,
Put her false teeth in the water,
    hung up her wig to dry,
Placed her false arm on the table,
    laid her false leg on the chair,
After the party was over,
    Bonnie was only half there!

Which was hilarious the first time I heard it, four years ago, and not the fifty-six times I've heard Cuddy bellow it in the last two days.

Why did I ever think it was a good idea to teach Cuddy that song in the first place? And why, oh, why did I have to run into Cuddy's mother while escaping from Mad Madge and her hooligan cousin Nincompoop?

Yes, Mad Madge is a girl. But she's unlike any other eleven-year-old girl I've ever seen. The only other person who comes close to her is my cousin Geri, and believe you me, that's not a good thing. Madge is mean and surly and uses words I've never heard before. Let's just say I'm highly suspicious of (a) her real age, and (2) her parents. I'm pretty sure one of them is a grizzly bear.

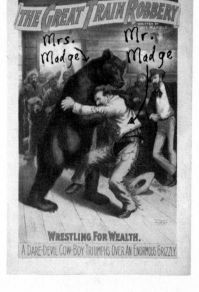

She is also fast. But not as fast as me. My heart was pumping as I zigzagged through the streets like a champ, making my getaway. I was as light-footed as a bare-knuckle boxer in the ring, and I was pretty sure Mad Madge couldn't catch me if she had wanted to.

Until, that is, I bumped into Mrs. Carlisle, a woman whose bones are so weak my slight nudge left her with a broken leg. That little accident also left me with the task of watching her son, Cuddy Carlisle, while she is on the mend and left my mama with the task of doing the Carlisles' laundry. For free.

"Also, Stan," Cuddy says, tugging on my sleeve, "if you didn't help watch me, Mother was going to have your mother pay for part of her medical bills, remember? Remember that part?"

There is no way Mama would be able to help pay anyone else's bills—we can barely pay our own. And when will I learn to keep my thoughts to myself instead of letting them flow through my lips like water from a well?

"I don't know when you'll learn that lesson, Stan," Cuddy says. His hands are red and sticky from the penny candy clenched in his pudgy fingers.

"C'mon, Cuddy," I sigh. "Let's go run those errands." I try to flatten the list Mrs. Carlisle gave me. It's long and will require at least four stops, which means Cuddy will talk to every single shop owner and customer and I won't get back to the boardinghouse to help Mama until all the boarders have eaten and all that's left for my growling stomach is a dry crust of bread and a pinch of salt.

"Here, Stan! You can have my candy!" Cuddy's hand juts into my face. The candy is covered with gullyfluff from his pocket and is glued to his hand like a sixth finger.

I'm no stranger to dirt or lint, but even I have my limits. "Um, no thanks, Cuddy," I say.

Kids.

"What did you say, Stan?" Cuddy runs to keep up with me.

I think quickly. I can't insult him. After all, I did make his mother an invalid. And even though he's only seven, calling him a kid can send him into a minor tantrum.

"Squids, Cuddy. I said 'squids.'"

"Why, Stan? Why were you talking about squids? Have you ever seen a squid? I know all about the giant squid! Do you want to hear about it?"

Like I'm going to believe that's real.

THE GIANT SQUID AT BAY.

I shake my head no, but it doesn't matter. Cuddy is going to tell me about the giant squid anyway.

"Mother says my uncle Cuthbert—that's who I was named after—traveled all over the world and that's why I can't ever sit still. I'm just like him. So my uncle Cuthbert found a giant squid once in Newfoundland. Do you know where that is, Stan?"

He never waits for me to answer.

"It's in Canada, Stan. Do you know where Canada is, Stan? Huh? Do you?"

I nod and turn down the street toward the mercantile, gazing out over the milky, half-frozen bay, trains and ships steaming up the gray sky. I'm trying to keep both of Cuddy's feet on the boardwalk and out of the dirty, muddy road; Cuddy's grandmother doesn't appreciate a dirty Cuddy.

Mama says my accident with Mrs. Carlisle could have been worse—keeping an eye on Cuddy is a small price to pay. If we had had to help with Mrs. Carlisle's medical bills, we would have ended up in the poorhouse. Or if the weather were warmer, I'd be required to cart Cuddy's mom around on a Carrycycle like Jim McMaster does with his grandmother, Old Mrs. McMaster. Although everyone knows he only does that so she'll keep him in her will.

Whee!

KALAMAZOO CARRYCYCLE

Just what it looks to be — the most comfortable vehicle in the world for an invalid to ride in. It will pay you to investigate it. The chair can be detached and a box put on for store delivery. The steering mechanism is a wonder. It is almost self-steering.

We also manufacture eighteen different styles of child's seats and parcel carriers for bicycles. Ask your dealer for Kalamazoo Carriers or write to us.

FOLDING PARCEL CARRIER

MANUFACTURED BY
KALAMAZOO CYCLE CO.,
KALAMAZOO, MICH.

I look over Mrs. Carlisle's list:

1. Toilet soap
2. One tooth polisher
3. Cocoa
4. Baking powder
5. Shaving stick
6. Pick up order from Steinberg's

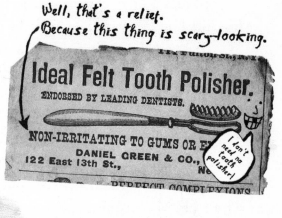

Well, that's a relief.
Because this thing is scary-looking.

Ideal Felt Tooth Polisher.
ENDORSED BY LEADING DENTISTS.
NON-IRRITATING TO GUMS OR E
DANIEL GREEN & CO.,
122 East 13th St.,

I don't need no tooth polisher!

Stop soap abuse!

Pears'
Soap

How has it come to pass that all the world insists on having Pears' Soap.
It is pure soap and nothing but soap—there is not a millionth part of free alkali in it. Established over 100 years, it has received the highest awards at every International Exhibition, from the first in London, 1851, to the last in Edinburgh, 1890.

What's in the lather?
If you use the so-called cheap kinds and most others, you may expect

If you use WILLIAMS' SHAVING SOAP you may count on

This looks messy.

Williams'
SHAVING SOAP.

THE UNIVERSAL POPULARITY
THE ONLY REAL SHAVING SOAPS

Buy this one.

We're directly in front of Steinberg's so we dodge a couple of horses and slide in to pick up Mrs. Carlisle's order.

We pass shelves of cotton fabric stacked to the ceiling, some ready-made trousers and dresses, and thread displayed like candy behind glass counters. Cuddy picks up a vase full of buttons.

"Look, Stan! Look! I can balance this on my head!" I rush over just in time to catch the vase before it crashes to the floor.

"Nice catch, Stan!" He tries to clap but somehow his hands get stuck. I set the vase carefully down on the counter, hoping no one notices how sticky it is, and I realize his candy is gone.

"Cuddy," I say, grabbing both his shoulders, "where is your candy?"

"I thtuck it in my mouth." He grins and juice runs down his chin. I quickly wipe it up with my coat sleeve.

"Hi, Stan! Hey there, Cuddy!" Mr. Steinberg says. I push Cuddy and his sticky self behind me, praying he doesn't touch anything. "You picking up Mrs. Carlisle's order?" I nod. "I'll have that ready for you straightaway."

"Do you know anything about giant squids, Mr. Steinberg?" Cuddy asks, peeking around my back. "Did you know they eat children and dogs?" he continues without waiting for a reply. Mr. Steinberg hands me a brown paper package and laughs.

"No, Cuddy. Can't say as I was aware of that fact," he says before turning to answer the telephone.

"C'mon, Cuddy." I tuck the package under my arm and head for the door.

"Oh! Wait just a moment, boys!" Mr. Steinberg yells. "That was Mrs. Carlisle. She has one more item for you."

"The squid my uncle Cuthbert found was bigger than this store and had eyes the size of dinner plates," Cuddy says.

Don't answer the phone! Nothing good can come from this.

"She said not to bother wrapping it," Mr. Steinberg says as he takes a corset—a *corset*—off a nearby mannequin and hands it to me. "I'm afraid it's the last one and we want to make sure not to bend it, now, don't we?"

I am appalled. These people expect me to walk down State Street carrying a woman's undergarment like it's an everyday occurrence? Where is their sense of decency? What is this world coming to?

What if someone sees me?

"Here, Cuddy," I say, thrusting the corset into his hands. I had forgotten how dirty they were until he reached out. I think he has three flies and a dog stuck to them. I jerk the corset away. If he ruins it, I will probably have to replace it, and with all our money going to fix up the boardinghouse, Mama would

• 9 •

certainly not understand if I had to buy some lady a new undergarment.

"C'mon, Cuddy," I say for the eleventh time since school got out. I snake my arm through the corset in an attempt to make it look like it's part of my coat, as if I have one very round, long sleeve. I try to convince myself no one will notice.

"That looks silly, Stan!" Cuddy yells from behind me. Three men turn around, and I feel my cheeks burn a path up to my ears. "You look like you have one giant arm. Like someone in the circus. Like a sideshow person. Have you ever gone to the circus, Stan? I have. I went to one in Chicago. There was a knife thrower and a tightrope walker and some trick monkeys. Mother wouldn't let me see the sideshows, but I saw a poster for a guy who could bend in half, and a teeny, tiny guy, and a lady with a beard. You look like you could be one of those people, Stan, don't you think? With that thing on your arm?"

For a minute I think about bendy men and hairy ladies. I actually do want to know more, but it is not a good idea to encourage Cuddy's talking—one minute it's the circus, the next it's his grandmother's gout.

I learned that lesson the hard way.

"Should we go into Kreuger's, Stan?"

I just want to get this entire day over with. I want to drop off Cuddy and this dadgum corset. . . .

"Watch your mouth, Stan. You said 'dadgum,' and Mother always says that's a swear. I won't tell her you said a swear, but you might want to be careful, because Reverend Elliot says swearing's a sin. You shouldn't swear, Stan."

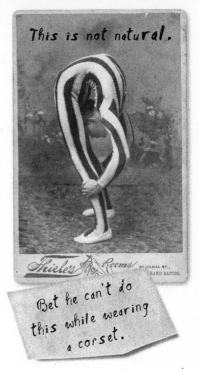

This is not natural.

Bet he can't do this while wearing a corset.

All I want to do is swear, but apparently even thinking of swearing can land me in a heap of trouble.

And then I see something up ahead that makes me stop in my tracks and want to utter every swearword I know.

"What in the blazes?" I mutter. I don't even care if Cuddy hears me.

Help me.

I'm this shocked.

"What was that? What did you say, Stan?" Cuddy stops next to me and catches the package from under my arm.

Carts fill the street, clopping down the semi-frozen ground, carrying goods and people through town. None of that is out of the ordinary.

"Did you see a giant squid, Stan?" Cuddy snorts and slaps his knee like he's told a great joke.

One wagon in particular has captured my attention like I'm looking through a camera and it's the only thing in focus.

It seems to speed toward us but takes a lifetime to get here. My ears feel full and my head swims. I recognize the driver, Uncle Carl, but he's not who I'm worried about. My breath catches as the wagon gets nearer. Is that who I think it is? A ramrod-straight spine. A nose so sharp it could cut glass. An old lady so mean I'm pretty sure even Vlad the Impaler would quake in his boots.

Fortunately, I'm wise to that woman's tricks. I square my shoulders and prepare myself for battle.

But then I see the most frightening sight of all. Peeking out of the wagon, under a heap of blankets, is a mess of unruly curls.

"Stan! I'm hungry!" Cuddy says.

For once, I'm not.

The old lady might be scary, but the person attached to that messy head of hair is downright dangerous.

She's been trying to kill me for years.

THE DEATH OF COLUMBUS.

CHAPTER 2

Hello! Hello! Anybody in there?" Cuddy waves his mother's package in my face.

I take it with my one free hand and steer Cuddy toward his house. My mind is still reeling, spinning through all the possible dangers that await me now that my evil granny and devious cousin are in town.

Who will try to do me in first? Granny with her disapproving stare and unrealistic expectations? Or Geri and her deadly medical diagnoses?

This year alone she's almost killed me with effluvia, spontaneous combustion, and tedium. Fortunately, I made it out alive—a less manly soul might not have been so lucky.

"Let's get you back home, Cuddy. I think it's time for your tea, isn't it?" I sigh, adjusting the corset higher on my shoulder.

"I sure hope so! I sure hope Grandmother has the tea and cookies ready, Stan. I'm about starved!" He rubs his belly.

The rest of our errands will have to wait, because I need to drop this child off and get back home before my worst nightmare throws all my belongings out the window onto the street, where wild dogs will carry them away.

Wild? No. Dogs with bad habits? Definitely.

"Wild dogs?" Cuddy says, his voice quavering. "Are there wild dogs around here, Stan?"

I know he already worries about dying from rabies and childbirth and lockjaw and Jumping Frenchmen of Maine syndrome. And while I realize I should immediately reassure him of the lack of wild dogs or his mother will kill me, probably by beating me with her crutch, I also realize Cuddy might be the perfect solution for what awaits me at home.

A JOLLY DOG.

Geri. Geri can diagnose Cuddy. They might be a match made in heaven.

"Where are the wild dogs, Stan? Eek!" Cuddy lunges toward me as Chuck Luebner's mutt, Teeny, waddles up to us. "Stan! Is that one? Is that blood dripping from its jaws?"

I lift the corset over my head. "No, Cuddy. That's Teeny.

You know Teeny. You let Teeny lick your hand about half an hour ago, remember?"

But Cuddy is long gone, scooting around the corner faster than I've ever seen his chubby legs move.

This wild dog story might actually be useful. Especially when I'm trying to get Cuddy to move faster than a turtle with a cane.

Which is always.

"Whatcha got there, Stan the Bedpan?"

I don't even have to turn around to know it's Mad Madge. She's the only one brave enough to call me a name. I should probably recommend a better one, like Stan the Wise Man or Stan the Sporting Man or even just Stan the Man, but I'm afraid to encourage her. Or talk to her at all. Also, I'm pretty sure she's with her cousin Nincompoop.

"What did you call me?" Nincompoop asks, stepping out from behind Madge.

I stand frozen to the spot. Cuddy is a block ahead of me and probably to the steps of his house by now. Maybe he'll realize I'm missing by tomorrow and come find my dead body underneath a lady's corset, stuck behind the Methodist Episcopal Church.

"Um." It's a good thing I'm so quick on my feet. Especially since I've yet to learn not to blurt things out before thinking. "I said, 'Hey, did you hear the scoop?'"

"Scoop? What's a scoop?" Nincompoop asks.

Mad Madge, however, perks up, her eyes wide with interest. "Do you have news, Stan?" she asks, leaning toward me while looking around like we share a secret.

"News?"

"Yes," Madge whispers. "You said you had a scoop." She reaches into her satchel, probably for some sort of weapon. I place the corset across my chest like a piece of armor.

A really sad piece of armor.

"So spill," Madge says as she pulls out a notepad and pencil.

I relax a bit. I'm 85.6 percent sure my corset can fend off her pencil. Also, I'm not too worried about Nincompoop—he's digging a finger in his ear, an activity that seems to require all of his attention.

Madge keeps staring at me. "Well? I don't have all day."

Well, what? What does she want from me?

Madge's shoulders drop and her eyes narrow. She takes a step closer. "You said you had a scoop. Now, what is this scoop you mentioned?" Her hand hovers over the paper as she waits for me to answer. "I want this scoop, Stan. It's important for me to know everything that goes on in this town." She pokes her pencil in my face like she's dotting an exclamation mark.

I sift through the past few minutes. Why does she think I have a scoop? Scoop. Scoop. Oh! Nincompoop! Mad Madge thinks I have news! Of course! I try to wave away that silly idea, but that's difficult to manage while holding a package and a corset.

Mad Madge's eyes turn to slits. "Oh, not going to share your news source, eh?"

I swallow hard. "No! No, I mean, I don't have any news!"

Mad Madge sighs and then, like the wick turned up on a lamp, brightens as she looks at me like I'm a gift to her from the Bully God.

There he is! Go beat him up!
(Except he's not a girl.)

"We have ways of making you talk," she says, taking a step toward me. "What's this on your arm?" Mad Madge knows perfectly well what this is on my arm.

"Um, it's a delivery, if you must know." I take a step backward, ready to make my getaway before Madge decides to throw me to the ground, wrap me up in the corset, and then tie me to a tree.

"What a great suggestion!" she says gleefully. "Nicholas! Grab him!" She moves aside but her timing is slightly off, and rather than getting out of Nincompoop's way, she backs into him. Nincompoop loses his footing, his finger still stuck in his ear, panicking like ants are caught in his brain and can't get out.

Which would be the most that brain has ever held, if you want to know the truth.

I'm a whiz at the truth, I don't mind saying. Unless I'm not telling it. Then I'm a whiz at little white lies. Which never hurt anybody.

Mad Madge looks serious for a moment and then says forcefully, "It's never okay to tell lies, Bedpan."

I'm getting moral advice from a gangster. That's how low I've sunk.

Nincompoop tries to regain his balance and steps onto Mad Madge's foot. She wobbles and grabs his arm, and they both fall into the trash piled up behind Murray Brothers' Grocery Store.

If I know anything, it's a good time to make an exit. I turn tail and head for Cuddy's house.

When I woke up this morning I never, ever in a million years would have thought this day would end up with me

STAN!
Come back here!
I'm not done with you!

running down the street wearing a corset, Mad Madge's hollers following me like dandelion fluff carried away by the wind.

I curve my path up the steps of the Carlisles' white house. Cuddy left the door wide open, something I'm certain to be blamed for.

Sure enough, I slow my breathing and look up into the face of Cuddy's grandmother, Mrs. Law, her gray hair pulled back so severely her eyebrows look surprised. Her arms are crossed.

In my experience this is not a good sign.

"What is not a good sign, Stanley?" Mrs. Law asks. Her lips are thin and straight and barely move.

I thrust the package toward her. "I said, 'Isn't today fine?' Yep. That's what I said, Mrs. Law. Ma'am. And how are you today?" I smile with all my teeth.

"I'll take this," she says, reaching for the corset. My arm aches from holding it up for so long.

"Why on earth did you carry it around on your arm?" she scoffs while pulling it off me. "Another desperate cry for attention? Hmmm?"

I don't say anything. I have been taught to respect my elders. Especially when they're really old.

Mrs. Law's expression tells me I've maybe said this last thing out loud. I swear I will never learn.

"So," I say, covering up, "what do you think? What are your opinions on the common cold?"

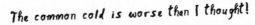

The common cold is worse than I thought!

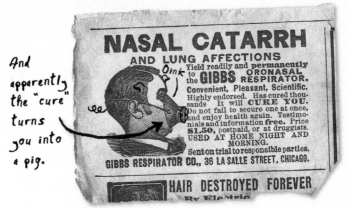

And apparently the "cure" turns you into a pig.

"Mrs. Carlisle would like to see you, Stanley. She's in the parlor." Mrs. Law then turns toward the kitchen and slams the door behind her.

I scrape my shoes on the mat and walk down the long hallway. The wood on the walls of the entryway is so shiny I can almost see myself in it, and the rug has strange patterns and colors—if I stare at it, I feel like the hero in *One Thousand and One Nights,* ready to fly off on his magic carpet.

Me

A really big lamp

The Carlisles' rug

Except his carpet flies off on exotic adventures, and mine just leads to a stuffy old parlor.

"Stan? Where are you, child?" I enter the room to find Mrs. Carlisle reclined on her sofa and dressed in so much fluffy white she could pass for one of those clouds you see only on hot summer days.

I can't imagine my own mama in such an outfit. It would be torn and covered in ash or grease from tending the stove or cooking meals for boarders.

"Stanley, have a seat," Mrs. Carlisle says. She directs me toward a chair across from her. At least I think it's a chair. It looks like something you could sit on if you had to.

Is this a chair or a slide?

THE SPANISH EASY CHAIR.

I get a little closer, and Mrs. Carlisle grimaces. "Uh, on second thought, why not stand? That might be a bit more comfortable for you." I look down at my hands twisting my coat. The knees of my knickers aren't really dirty, just worn in spots, although I might remember Mama yelling this morning, "Come back here, young man! The seat of those trousers is so filthy I think you're growing potatoes back there!" But I was late and couldn't be bothered.

"That's fine, Mrs. Carlisle. I sure wouldn't mind taking a load off these feet of mine." I maneuver toward the sunshiny yellow chair, but that woman is quick. She whips out

We need to cure this woman before she kills someone with her crutches.

her crutch and sticks it in my chest so fast, if it were a revolver, I would be dead.

"No. I insist you stand, Stanley." She smiles and slowly places the crutch at her side. "So I noticed that Cuddy seemed to have had quite the adventure today. He arrived home decidedly less put-together than when he left." She stares at me.

"What was he missing, Mrs. Carlisle?" I'm confused. I am pretty sure when he got back home he had both arms and legs and his head attached. Now, there were those few minutes while I was fending off a gangster attack when I suppose something could have happened. . . .

"Oh, no, no, Stanley. It's just that he was a bit unkempt. And dirty. And his trousers were ripped. And he was ranting on and on about perhaps having contracted rabies?"

Cuddy always overreacts.

This dog just ate some soap. Which explains the bubbly mouth. (I should know. I've tasted my share of soap.)

I shrug. "Oh, that Cuddy," I say with a smile. "He does have quite the imagination, now, doesn't he?" My face feels stiff. I'm sure I'll be fired from this job any minute and have to tell Mama that it's time to pack up and leave for the poorhouse. I'll need to quit school to work down at the docks or out at the lumberyard, or perhaps I'll need to become a member of Mad Madge's gang and start hitting people over the head and stealing their pocket change. Or perhaps the corset will be my weapon of choice.

"Excuse me, Stanley." Mrs. Carlisle leans toward me. "Did you hear what I just said?"

I look at her blankly. I guess I didn't hear what she just said.

"Cuddy seems happier than I've seen him in months. Ever since, well, ever since the fall when we moved here. So I just want to thank you for taking care of him. Perhaps my broken leg was a blessing in disguise."

Whew. I breathe deeply and shake out my arms. I had been holding them stiffly to my sides like I was some sort of tin soldier. Truth be told, these people make me as nervous as a couple of worms at a bird convention. I should have known Mrs. Carlisle would want to thank me; why, who knows what would happen to Cuddy if I weren't here to show him the ropes? He'd probably end up some sort of sad mama's boy spending all of his days listening to opera and darning socks.

Mrs. Carlisle smiles, and I look for a place to sit in case she wants to tell me more nice things.

"Uh, no need to sit," Mrs. Carlisle says, her hand on the crutch. "I just wanted to give you tomorrow's list and ask if perhaps you could see to it that Cuddy stays a bit cleaner from now on."

I nod and take the list. I'm going to have to add some things from today's list, too. I hope she doesn't notice.

"I also want to give you this, Stanley." Mrs. Carlisle holds out one shiny silver twenty-five-cent piece.

Is this a trick?

"Initially I needed you to watch Cuddy because of my unfortunate situation." She flounces her fluffy white arm around her broken leg. "But you have done quite a nice job, and for that, I would like to hire you to watch Cuddy after school and run some errands. Mr. Carlisle and I feel you've earned it."

I take the coin between my two fingers. My very own money, money I can use to help support Mama and me.

"We will pay you twenty-five cents a week," she says. "As long as you do a good job."

Pfft. I am a whiz at doing a good job, I don't mind saying. Unless we're talking about schoolwork. Or washing the dishes. Or maybe shoveling. But those jobs don't count.

Mrs. Carlisle turns away dismissively. I bow as I leave the room, backing right into Mrs. Law. When I whip around, she has Cuddy's trousers pressed into my face.

"Young Mr. Slater," she says. "The next time you deliver Master Carlisle to me in such atrocious condition, you will either take the time to clean his clothing yourself or buy the child a new suit." She flings the pants to the side as if she's a matador and I'm a bull.

But sure as the sun rises in the North, even the meanest bull in existence would drop dead from the combination of that woman's hot breath and cold, cold eyes.

I'm a whiz at science, I don't mind saying.

I turn and dash out the door, slap my cap on my head, check both ways to make sure Mad Madge and her crony cousin aren't waiting to ambush me, and skedaddle home before I even take the time to think about what awaits me there.

Which is a mistake.

Choo choo

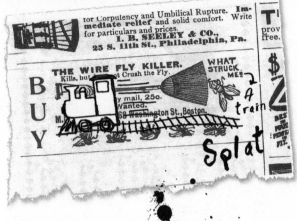

CHAPTER 3

I scoot through the back alley, past the shops and between houses, avoiding dogs and always on the lookout for the train. Mama says her biggest fear is that I won't be paying attention and will end up *splat!* like a fly in a wire fly killer.

I tried to explain that I probably wouldn't be splattered on the tracks, but rather thrown off to the side, my arms to the right and my legs to the left, but she didn't seem to want to discuss that scenario.

I don't know why she even brought it up.

The track runs behind the boardinghouse. Mama doesn't like me out there because of the train, obviously, but also because of the people who tend to gather there, fellows who are generally just down on their luck. Guys like Eugene "Genius" Malone. He's not a bad sort. In fact, he's a lot less dangerous than other people I know, specifically someone whose name rhymes with *scary* and *berry* and *cherry*.

That would be Geri.

This is a perfect example of the saying, "You can't judge a book by its cover."

Safe

Deadly dangerous

"Yo! Clem!" I jump to high heaven as a dusty figure emerges from behind the trees and dead leaves lining the banks of the railroad tracks. It's Eugene. No matter how many times I remind him my name is Stan, he insists on calling me Clem, which doesn't seem very genius to me.

"What's the news round town?" he asks, brushing off his pants. They don't look any cleaner.

I pause for a moment. It seems like something must have happened today. Something that knocked the wind out of me. Something unusual that made this day stand out from all the other days.

"Hmmm. Nothing new, Gene. Can't say as if today was much different than yesterday, to tell you the truth," I say sadly. We need a little excitement around here.

Gene scratches his whiskery chin. "Well, well. Excitement's not all it's cracked up to be, ya know. Sometimes just keeping on the straight and narrow, being happy with what you've been given, appreciating the little things . . . yep, sometimes that's the best plan."

"Ha, Eugene! Good one!" I bend over, laughing. I hear tell that Eugene Malone used to be one of the richest men in town, a regular dandy with his fancy suits and fashionable hats. Mrs. Law, of all people, said he was once "quite the catch." Which worries me a bit for Gene's safety, to be honest. I can't imagine what would happen if she actually caught him.

I get serious for a second. "And it's Stan, Gene. *Stan!*"

Gene just nods as he slowly picks at his teeth. "I speak the truth, Clem. Mind my words. You can't pay money for peace of mind." He tips his cap and meanders on down the track toward town. I happen to know he's headed off to see Reverend Elliot at the Methodist Episcopal Church. Gene eats with Reverend Elliot once a week. I'm pretty sure it's his act of charity, because the good reverend sure can talk, and he loves to go on and on about how no one appreciates him.

She flung herself on her knees beside the bed, and buried her face in her hands.

Page 15.

"Don't even tell me you are berating the honorable name of a man of the cloth," says a chilling voice behind me. I'm afraid to turn around. "I pray for your very soul, Stanley Arthur Slater."

I thought this ghastly woman and her evil, manners-minding ways were still at the lumber camp Mama and I left a month ago. I thought we were rid of her when we got on that wagon to start life anew in St. Ignace, a life of adventure and derring-do, not the boring existence of your average law-abiding citizen.

If she had her way, I'd be like Marshall Curtis, a boy who just so happens to be our teacher Miss Wenzel's very favorite student. I know this because she always calls on him and laughs at his pathetic jokes. Probably because she feels sorry for him. And probably because he always does what she asks him to do. And his trousers are always clean and pressed. And his assignments are always neat, and the girls always give him valentines even when it's not St. Valentine's Day.

He's intolerable.

"I actually met Marshall when we stopped downtown for supplies. He's quite a considerate young man. And handsome, too." That voice makes me feel the same way I did when I tried using Mama's electric hairbrush—tingly. And not in a good way. I close my eyes and force myself not to answer or turn around. If I don't see her, maybe she will cease to exist.

This is a woman who thinks a bit of swearing will doom your soul and poor manners will ensure a future in the pokey. A woman who has the imagination of a flea and the brain to match.

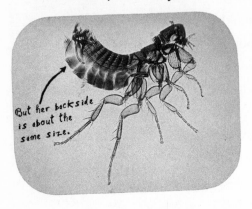

She actually has more hair and fewer legs.

But her backside is about the same size.

A woman who insists I call her Granny.

"Oh, Stanley." Her words drip disappointment. "I see our time apart has only served to make you stray down the path of juvenile delinquency. I don't know with whom you've been spending time, but they are obviously of questionable character, judging by the behavior I've just witnessed. We are all known by the company we keep, and if you surround yourself with people who fail to respect a man of the cloth, swear like sailors, and have poor manners, you will become more like them."

How long can I stand here without turning around? And if I wait long enough, will she leave?

"Also, who were you talking to before I came out? That man looked like he had just rolled through a pile of manure while eating a handful of dirt."

"Granny!" I've had more than enough of her old-fashioned, small-minded ways. "That, for your information, is a man down on his luck." I swing around to confront her. For someone who constantly tells me to love my neighbor, respect my elders, and be kind to all living things, she sure doesn't practice what she preaches. And I've had it. "That man is a genius, I'll have you know!" I actually am not sure he really is a genius. I think maybe someone just called him that because "genius" sounds funny with the name Eugene, and then it stuck. At least that's how I come up with my nicknames. Like Stan the Man.

Except that one is true.

(I'm a whiz at animals, I don't mind saying.)

Granny sucks in her cheeks.

"He just happens to have fallen on some hard times, Granny."

"He looks a bit familiar. What's his name?" Granny asks.

"Eugene. Eugene Malone," I answer cautiously. I wonder why she's so curious.

Her eyes widen, and I swear I hear her thoughts click into place like tumblers in a safe. "That's Eugene? My Eugene?" Granny grasps the neck of her dress and bites her lip.

"Um," I say. This is awkward. "I'm not sure he's yours, Granny." Could Granny be sweet on Eugene?

Ew.

Granny's face flushes. "Um." She straightens herself and her dress. "I just meant, I think I knew him once."

I nod. "So did Mrs. Law," I say.

"That old bat did not know Eugene like I did," Granny snarls.

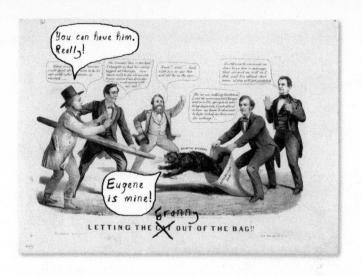

LETTING THE ~~CAT~~ Granny OUT OF THE BAG!!

"When did you know Mrs. Law? Or Eugene?" This is a surprising turn of events.

"We happened to attend school together."

"What the heck? You went to school?"

Granny pinches my arm. She's quicker than a bullfrog snatching a bug, and her pinch really hurts, even through my clothes. "Watch your mouth! I've got my eye on you, young man."

"I meant, where did you go to school, Granny?" I rub my arm as Granny adjusts her apron. She pushes me into the boardinghouse.

Granny is quicker than you'd think.

"I attended school here, Stanley. It's where I grew up. Do you ever pay attention to anything?"

This woman is insulting, exaggerates, and has no faith in her grandson. I open my mouth to respond, but I can't remember what she just said. Granny flattens her lips, closes her eyes, and heads to the kitchen, sighing loudly.

Once inside, I hear the low pitch of a man's voice and I remember Uncle Carl is here. That's a good thing. It's always a good thing when another man is around, because all too often I am outnumbered. I wonder if Uncle Carl has brought me any surprises, maybe a new jackknife or the newest Frank Leslie magazine.

As I unbutton my overcoat, however, I spy something that would strike fear in the heart of even a brave lion tamer. A girl's coat. One I would recognize anywhere.

How could I have forgotten? Geri. Geri is in my house.

Last time I saw Geri, we were saying good-bye at the lumber camp. I assumed she would be helping out during the river drive before she and her parents returned to Chicago.

I also short-sheeted her bed and put salt pork grease in one of her stockings. And I might have glued together some pages of her medical book.

In my defense, at the time I thought she had been playing pranks on me for three months before that and I was just returning the favor.

Unfortunately, the prankster turned out to be Granny. And I didn't have time to undo the pranks before we left to come here.

Plus, I thought it was funny.

Now I'm not so sure.

I tiptoe into the parlor. Geri is definitely the type of person who will return a favor. Or a prank. And she's devious and sneaky and makes very tasty bacon.

Do I smell bacon?

The parlor appears to be clear except for Old Mr. Glashaw, who doesn't get along with his wife and thinks his son is a namby-pamby.

A HIRED GIRL

THE BIG FARCE COMEDY SUCCESS

Some people just don't have a sense of humor.

"WATCH HER,

SHE'S FUNNY."

No, no, she's not.

His son *is* a namby-pamby. He yells at us kids every day for running across his yard and scaring his dog, Foofy. I don't blame Old Mr. Glashaw one bit for not wanting to live with his wife and son.

When I'm old and don't have to listen to anyone, I'm going to live at a boardinghouse and have someone make my dinners and wash my clothes and change my sheets.

"How is that any different from your life now?" a scratchy voice asks. It's coming from the room behind me through a crack in the door. I shuffle over and peek inside.

I don't recognize the person lying in the bed, covered with three worn blankets. I do, however, seem to vaguely remember a hat like that.

Hey! That's *my* hat! My very favorite lucky hat. It's all coming back to me. Stinky Pete gave it to me; he said it made me look manly.

"If it meant so much to you, why did you forget it at camp?" The body rolls over like it's lying on porcupine quills, slowly and gingerly.

I squint. "Geri?"

She nods, her eyes closed like even the dim light hurts. Her hair curls around the hat every which way, and her skin looks like wax, hollowed and shadowed in all the wrong places.

She looks bad, but I'm

still skeptical. This is a girl who has been known to diagnose me with all sorts of deadly diseases and get me in so much trouble that one time I had to run away from both Conrad McAllister and Lydia Mae at the same time. For entirely different reasons.

It was quite the ruckus.

Geri is always creating ruckuses, so it's understandable why I'm a bit cautious. But when I hear her cough, her breath shallow and raspy, I know this is not a joke and scoot myself right out of the room.

I am not a very good nurse.

Does Mama know Geri is in the back bedroom? And that Granny is here? And that Granny is sweet on Gene?

The front door slams. I see Uncle Carl leaving the house with some man who practically tippy-toes down the sidewalk toward State Street.

I know that tippy-toeing guy.

How do I know that guy?

He turns toward town, a spring in his step as he tilts his cap to a lady trotting by in a carriage, his jaw a-flapping at Uncle Carl like a worried bird's wings.

It's Mr. Archibald Crutchley. My enemy. My nemesis. I thought I had left him back at that lumber camp, too.

Why, oh, why are all these people following me? And why,

oh, why is it all the people I wanted to leave behind as I started my new life? A life of manliness, danger, and adventure?

My shoulders slump. I wonder what that man is doing here. I know he and Granny are two peas in a pod and just about as mushy.

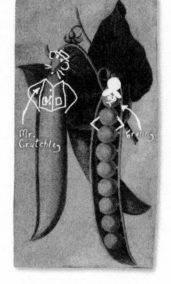

Plus, I trust them about as far as I can throw them. And while I've never tried throwing Mr. Crutchley, I did try picking Granny up once, only to show her how strong I was becoming. It didn't end so well. She didn't budge one inch and gave me a black eye with her rolling pin.

She claims it was an accident, but who hits someone just because his arms are around your legs and he's trying to lift you off the floor ? And maybe that fellow just so happened to sneak behind you quietly and you were surprised and reacted without thinking.

Hmmm. Maybe that wasn't such a bright idea.

I meander toward the kitchen but stop as soon as I hear the conversation going on.

It's about money. It's always about money.

Or me. And my lack of manners and poor judgment.

"Dear, all I'm suggesting is don't rule him out," Granny says.

"I'm not deciding one way or the other," Mama replies over the clanging of pots. "I'm simply not convinced."

"Convinced of what?" Granny scoffs. "You're going to lose everything if your pride gets in the way of your heart. You don't have that luxury. And was he not a complete gentleman and somewhat charming to boot?"

Who are they talking about? If it weren't Granny's voice, I'd think they were referring to me since I'm known to be quite the charmer. And quite the gentleman, I don't mind saying.

"I will admit that Mr. Crutchley was surprisingly entertaining."

What? *What?* "Entertaining" and "Mr. Crutchley" go together about as well as "Sweet" and "Granny."

"Well, that's a start, dear," Granny says.

This is what "entertaining" looks like.

This is what it feels like to spend time with Mr. Crutchley.

"But I'm not planning on marrying him, Mother. How many times do we have to discuss this?" Mama adds.

"Until you get some sense, apparently. Archie is the perfect solution to your problem," Granny replies. "If you don't bring in some money and soon, this place is going to the bank. And then where will you and Stan be? There's no room for you at your sister's, and you know with Stanley's poor judgment, if you move him to Chicago, he'll just fall in with some gang and end up a derelict or beggar on the street."

Hello! I can hear you!

Except I don't want her to know I can hear her. Sometimes, when spying, you have to make tough choices. Also, I have a paying job now. I can take care of my mama, thank you very much. I pull the quarter from my pocket and eye its shininess.

"We're not talking about an extra twenty-five cents here or there," Granny continues. All of a sudden my quarter doesn't seem so shiny. "Archie has real funds to invest in order to make this place a success. Why not at least consider him? For Stanley's sake?"

Mama sighs. "Fine. Fine." She sounds exasperated. "I won't rule him out. If things get that desperate, I guess."

What? No! Rule him out! That sorry excuse for a man can't marry my mama!

I'm going to have to scrounge up more money. And fast.

How can I scrounge up some more money fast?

I slyly clear my throat to announce my presence. I don't want them to think I was eavesdropping.

"Were you eavesdropping?" Granny accuses, peering around the door frame.

One thing I cannot forgive is someone accusing me of something I certainly did not do.

Another thing I cannot forgive is someone accusing me of something I certainly *did* do.

"Of course not!" I scoff. "I didn't hear a word about that awful Mr. Crutchley or money problems or how you are sweet on Eugene Malone."

"What?" Granny huffs. "Why, I . . ."

"Hey! Did you two happen to notice that Geri is sick?" I ask. I'm really glad I can bring this to their attention since they've obviously been quite neglectful of her health.

Granny shifts her hips and stares at me. "Oh, really?"

I nod. "Really. She's in the back room, coughing and hacking like the air is thick as honey." Geez-oh-pete. Am I the only one with any sense around here?

Also, where is the honey? I'm hungry.

"Stan," Mama says. "Watch your language."

"Yes, Mama," I say, holding my breath. Is that all? Am I going to get pinched? Am I going to get punished for saying "Geez-oh-pete"? Criminy, I didn't even know I said that out loud.

Granny glares at me, her arms crossed.

Did I say *that* out loud, too? I'd better change the subject while I have the chance. "So! Would you like me to do anything for Geri? Mr. Glashaw? Was that Mr. Crutchley I saw leaving the house?" I say casually. Just uttering his name makes me grind my teeth.

"Yes," Granny answers. "And he'll be back for dinner, so mind your manners." She shakes a rolling pin in my face. I flinch. That rolling pin and I are not the best of friends.

"And let Geri rest. She's come down with a touch of pleurisy. There's no room for illness on a river drive and the poor Chicago air is no better, so we're going to nurse her back to health here. Your job is to leave her alone, young man," Granny warns.

I salute her. But I do it behind her back. If she saw me,

"INDEPENDENCE DAY" OF THE FUTURE.

I'm pretty sure that rolling pin and I would be reacquainted right quick.

I tiptoe over to Geri's door. There's something strangely eerie and exciting about going where you're not supposed to go.

Which is exactly why I always end up in those places.

Not really the reputation I'm going for

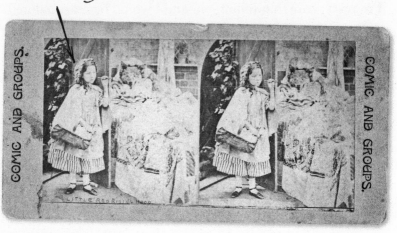

CHAPTER 4

P sst! Geri!" I whisper.

"Stan?" Her voice sounds like the word is scraping her throat.

"Good! You're awake!" I shuffle into the room and close the door, cringing when it squeaks.

Geri's eyes are closed. That's really all I can see of her under the pile of blankets and my hat.

I'm sure my recent hard luck is completely due to not having my good-luck charm firmly on my head.

I want my hat back. My ears have been cold for the past month, and I refuse to wear Mama's pink hat. She claims it's red, but she would be wrong. One time wearing that hat and

I'd never live it down. My nickname would probably end up being Little Red Riding Stan, and that's the least manly nickname in the history of nicknames.

"I know you're faking," I say, pulling up a chair.

No one has this much hair on his face.

Fake

Real

It doesn't get any more real than a cowboy.

Geri doesn't respond. I've never known her to be so quiet. I poke her cheek; she grimaces and pulls away like her skin hurts.

"You don't have to fake it with me, Geri," I say again, only this time I'm not so hissy and I actually hope she replies with some sort of comment, or at least tells me I'm dying of a weird illness like Jumping Frenchmen of Maine syndrome.

"Boo," she whispers halfheartedly. I look at her like she's a few gunmen short of a posse.

"That's all you've got?" I am starting to worry, to be honest.

Her eyes are still closed, her breathing heavy. She wets

Catarrh, Neuralgia & Headache

No More!
Well, this seems easy to fix!

Bonus! Maybe we can fix her head, too!

CUSHMAN'S MENTHOL INHALER.

CURES DISEASES OF THE HEAD INCLUDING
HAY-FEVER, COLDS & BRONCHITIS.
MANF'D BY H.D. CUSHMAN, THREE RIVERS, MICH

her lips and says, "You don't have Jumping Frenchmen of Maine syndrome, or you would have startled when I said, 'Boo,'" she explains.

I laugh. No one would have startled with that boo. Even a newborn baby wouldn't have been afraid. Which means one of two things: (a) I might be dying of Jumping Frenchmen of Maine syndrome, or (2) Geri is dying.

"I'm not dying, but I am quite sick. The doctor says it's pleurisy, but I think it's a bad case of catarrh." She swallows like a rock is stuck in her mouth.

"Is it catchy?" I ask, pushing against the back of the chair. The last thing I need is a deadly case of catarrh.

I can't even pronounce the word, for Pete's sake.

"Stanley!" I jump. Probably because I have Jumping Frenchmen of Maine syndrome.

"Probably not," Granny says, lifting me up by my ear. "But you will have Sore Bottom of Michigan syndrome if you don't heed my words and leave Geri alone." I notice the rolling pin in her other hand and a smirk on Geri's face.

Granny shuts the door behind us. "Now go to your room until we call you down for dinner. And I mean it. Leave. Geri. Alone." She points a finger right at my nose. "She needs the rest, and we don't need you getting sick as well."

I'm not so sure it isn't too late. It would be just like Geri to try to kill me even while she's stuck in bed.

I tromp up the stairs to the room I share with Mama. Some new magazines lie on my cot, probably a present from Uncle Carl. I flip through them and think about my unexciting day. I wish I were back at the lumber camp with my people. I hate to admit it, but I miss my friend Stinky Pete. He was probably my best friend.

I turn the page. I'll bet Stinky Pete misses me, too. He's probably wondering what I've been up to. He probably doesn't know what to do with himself now that he doesn't have anyone to play euchre or poker or checkers with. He's probably twiddling his thumbs and losing his ability to carry on a conversation.

I try to lose myself in a story called "Snatched from Death." I could have written that story; Lord knows I've had my share of near-death encounters.

This could have happened to me.

This, too!

Or this!

I'm just at the good part—Explosions! Dynamite! Fainting women and screaming children!—when a loose page falls on my lap, reminding me of my very major problem.

We are dead broke. And even though my twenty-five cents a week may help, it's gone after a bag of flour and a pound of bacon. I know Mr. Crutchley could buy the entire Mulcrone Meat Market and still have money left over to buy two farms and a lifetime supply of pickles. And that just might be enough to convince Mama to marry him.

If she's desperate.

This is exactly what Mr. Crutchley looks like.

Mr. Ratley

CHAPTER 5

Mr. Crutchley pulls out Mama's chair. His every movement is squeaky and twitchy like a rat's whiskers. I glare at him like I'm shooting bullets at his chest. With my eyes. My bullet-shooting eyes.

Not in a violent way. Just in a way that would make the fellow leave immediately to track down a doctor who would give him many, many painful stitches and he would lose his memory and forget my mama ever existed.

Geri can do the stitching.

You can hardly see the scar where she stitched me up.

Granny stands over me with a bowl of mashed potatoes. Her mouth is as flat as the metal ruler the principal uses to swat kids' behinds.

Not that I know anything about that.

Mr. Crutchley's head tilts and Mama sits midscooch on her chair. She looks at the ceiling the way she does when she's either trying not to yell at me or praying she doesn't kill me before I can prove the gray hairs on her head were all worth it.

I know this because she reminds me again and again.

"You are giving me many, many gray hairs on this head, Stanley Slater. Tell me again why it's worth it," she says.

She actually doesn't have any gray hairs.

I pull out my chair and sit down, fork in one hand, knife in the other.

"Good food, good meat, good Lord, let's eat!" I say, ready to dig in. But no one else moves. All three of them are staring at me. Am I missing something?

"Stanley. Please apologize to Mr. Crutchley. Immediately." Granny's voice is as clipped as Mrs. Glashaw's prized miniature poodle, Foofy.

"Sorry?" I say. But truthfully, I'm not sure what I'm sorry for.

"For hoping he'd lose his memory and need a doctor?" Granny sets down the bowl and wipes her hands on her apron.

Oh. That.

"Um, sorry," I say. I'm not sorry, but those potatoes are drowning in melted butter and sprinkled with salt and I *am* sorry I have to share them with Mr. Crutchley.

"Stan!" Mama says.

"I said, 'I am sorry my prayer didn't include Mr. Crutchley,'" I say quickly. I hope some mention of religion will get me off the hook. These people are suckers for some religious talk, tell you what.

"Oh! Well! That's nice of you, son." Mama bows her head. Mr. Crutchley shuffles quickly to help Granny with her chair before sidling up to the table himself. They bow their heads.

"Stanley," Granny says.

Do they expect me to say grace?

My mouth is full of potatoes. I quickly swallow and clear my throat. "Good food. Good meat. Good Lord. Let's eat,"

I pray. I say each part slowly and seriously. That's how Reverend Elliot always prays—really, really slowly. So slowly I almost fall asleep in church.

Mama ahems. I look up to see her looking at me. Her eyes should be closed! I'm saying grace here! She widens her eyes and flicks her head in Mr. Crutchley's direction. Why is she doing that?

Oh! I said I wished my prayer had included Mr. Crutchley!

"Um. Um," I say. "Um. Dear God, also, if you could remember Mr. Crutchley and, um, maybe bestow upon him some more hair." Mama accidentally kicks me under the table.

"And maybe help him grow all over. He's kind of short for a real man," I add.

SILVER SPUR

BUSH, THE Tree-Planter

I think he might appreciate more hair.

He's a little taller than this.

But only a little.

I nod my head, my eyes closed. I am getting into this prayer thing! I'm starting to see why Reverend Elliot likes to go on and on so much in church!

"And if you could perhaps make his breath smell better . . ."

"Amen!" Granny interrupts. "Archibald, would you like some stew?"

"Hey!" I say. I think it must be some sort of sin to interrupt a person while he is praying for someone who obviously needs a lot of praying for.

"Youch!" Mama kicks me again. I'm starting to think she's kicking me on purpose.

"Here," she says, handing me a plate. "Take this to Geri." I reach for the food and do as I'm told.

I'm a whiz at doing what I'm told, I don't mind saying. Unless I'm told to do something I don't really want to do. Then I'm a whiz at NOT doing what I'm told.

Either way, I'm pretty amazing.

I sneak into Geri's room. I can tell she's sleeping by the rasp in her chest as she breathes. It's wheezy and steady at the same time. Only part of her face is showing under all the blankets.

I set the food down on the chair, the one I saw Granny sitting in earlier today. She held a cool rag to Geri's cheek and kissed her forehead to check her temperature.

Remind me never to get that sick.

Geri's eyes are shut, of course. They sink into her face like they're melting into her skull. Her skin is almost see-through; even her freckles seem faded.

She hardly seems like the same girl who told me I was dying of yellow fever just a couple of months ago. Or dared me to stick my tongue to the frozen light post in front of our house in Manistique. She left me there, and I couldn't move or yell for help and would probably still be there today if Mama hadn't found me and loosened my tongue with some warm water.

No, this hardly seems like the same person. I think I prefer the Geri with a bit more life in her.

I leave her room, my hand on my growling stomach. I don't want to wake her, and I certainly don't want to hear how my growling stomach could be a symptom of some deadly disease.

That's all I need.

As I get closer to the kitchen, I hear Mr. Crutchley blabbering on and on, and an occasional "Oh, you don't say!"

from Granny, which only seems to encourage him. I slow down. I'm hungry, but I'm in no hurry to spend a perfectly good dinner with someone like Mr. Archibald Crutchley. He's enough to ruin someone's appetite.

As if that were possible.

"Well, I'm not one to bring up money matters," Mr. Crutchley says, "especially around the fairer sex." He snorts. "But I am more than capable of helping with the boardinghouse, Mrs. Slater, should you allow me to." I can practically hear him patting his little tuft of hair and straightening his tie. I peek around the door. He looks smug, like someone waiting for an award or like Marshall Curtis when Miss Wenzel holds his paper up in front of the class as an example of neatness.

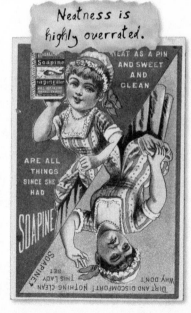

Mr. Crutchley glances between Mama and Granny. Granny's eyes flash, and her leg taps the floor. She might as well just yell "Cha-ching!" like a cash register making a sale.

Mama, on the other hand, keeps shoveling food in her mouth, as if she won't have to say anything if her mouth stays full.

Hey! I know that trick! I use it all the time. Especially when I'm having lunch next to Mad Madge. I've never known someone to ask so many nosy questions, and I never know if what I say will set her off. Also, she can make a regular, old pencil look like a very threatening weapon.

"Well, now!" Granny's voice brings me back to the present. Her voice has that sparkle to it that only shows up when Mr. Crutchley is present. "That's a lovely offer! Isn't it, Alice?"

Mama swallows. Hard. She places her fork solidly on the table and stands up with a long exhale. "I hope to make a go of it myself, thank you very much, Mr. Crutchley." I know that tone of voice. It's the same one she uses when I come home with bad marks from school or a note from the principal.

To be fair, the worms on Mad Madge's desk weren't only my idea. In fact, they weren't my idea at all. Cuddy wanted to dig up night crawlers for fishing later that week and so my pockets were full of them. I just needed somewhere to store them for a minute or two. Or five. And Mad Madge's desk seemed empty. And wormless.

It was an accident.

Only the principal and Mama didn't quite see it that way. And the tone of voice she's using right now is the exact same one she used that day.

Although for some reason I don't think she's going to send Mr. Crutchley to his room without any supper and make him write an apology to Mad Madge.

A DESTRUCTIVE WORM.

Maybe the horse is the gift!

Granny jumps into the conversation. "But we won't look a gift horse in the mouth, Archibald!" She lays a hand on Mama's shoulder. "Let's just see at the end of the summer how our finances are, shall we, dear?"

Mama seems like she wants to reply; her mouth hangs open, words lying on her tongue, waiting to leap all over Mr. Crutchley and his hare-brained idea.

He is a ridiculous excuse for a human being.

Granny leans close to Mama and whispers something I can't quite make out, but I swear she mentions my name. Mama shuts her mouth and nods. "Um." She hesitates, looking at her shoes. "Um, yes, Mr. Crutchley, although I do hope to make it on my own without any help, if need be, come September I would welcome your offer." She smiles at him tightly.

Mr. Crutchley practically dances out of his clean, pointy shoes. "That's wonderful! Oooh! So wonderful!" He claps his fingertips together. He can't even clap the right way.

"Now, Archibald, let me see you out," Granny says as Mama's shoulders drop. I step into the hallway, where I can still hear but can't be seen. Granny's hand rests on Mr. Crutchley's back, their heads almost touching. I can barely hear them, but I hear enough.

"Marriage is inevitable," Granny says.

"She'll need the money," Mr. Crutchley replies.

Granny nods. "Stan," she says. That word I hear loud and clear.

"Boarding school," Mr. Crutchley says.

Of course I could have misheard everything. That may have happened before. Once. Or five times.

Granny *could* have said, "Your carriage is terrible."

And Mr. Crutchley *could* have said, "I agree whole-heartedly."

I know they were talking about this.

LILY BUFKINS BECOMES MRS. STRIPES.

Or I suppose they could have been talking about this. Marriage. Carriage. They're really easy to get mixed up.

But I'm positive I heard "Stan." And "boarding school." Three words that should never be said together.

I need to act. Soon. I need to find a quick way of making money so Mr. Archibald Crutchley is not part of my not-so-distant future. And is definitely part of my far-flung past.

But how?

Get me out of here!

Take my word for it:
sometimes things can smell too good.

CHAPTER 6

I'm going to be rich. Rich, rich, richie rich," says a very determined voice next to me. I look up to find Mad Madge plopped down much too closely at the picnic table; her black hair, neatly plaited in two braids, shines in the noontime sun. She's so close I can't help noticing she smells surprisingly good, like bacon.

Mad Madge peers at me from the corner of her eye. "Are you sniffing me?"

I don't like her tone. It sounds like she's accusing me of something.

"Pfft. No," I scoff. "I think I have a cold." I sniff a few more times to throw her off track.

I usually go home for lunch, but today I didn't feel like it. Too many women telling me what to do—Stan, wash your hands! Stan, clean your fingerprints off the glass! Stan, pick up your clothes! Stan, you can't wear those dirty pants! Stan, take a bath! Stan, clean out the tub! Stan, wipe your feet! Stan, sweep the parlor!

What do they want from me?

Mad Madge's lunch pail gives me about two inches of room to sit, but I will admit, I'm a bit afraid to touch it in case it reminds her how much she really doesn't like me and then I end up wearing the pail as a new hat.

Mad Madge moves the bucket to the ground and I relax a little. She doesn't seem so mad here at lunch.

"Where is your goon?" I ask through a mouthful of cheese.

"Excuse me?" I take it back. Mad Madge still seems mad.

I swallow slowly. I think I swallowed my cheese all in one hunk. "Umm . . . I said, 'Who's got a spoon?'" Madge looks down at my lunch. I have another hunk of cheese, some bread slathered with butter, and a piece of Mama's pound cake.

"Why do you need a spoon?"

"Umm, I like to eat my bread with a spoon?" I am a whiz at improvising, I don't mind saying. Leah Tettinger hands me a spoon. I am not a whiz at eating bread with a spoon, however. It's hard to scoop out the bread without making a mess of crumbs.

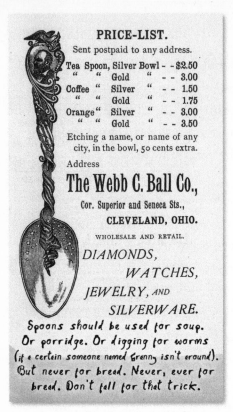

Spoons should be used for soup.
Or porridge. Or digging for worms
(if a certain someone named Granny isn't around).
But never for bread. Never, ever for
bread. Don't fall for that trick.

Madge smirks between bites of her sandwich.

"Stan! Stan!" Cuddy yells from the doorway. He's heading into the school with his class. "Wait till you see what I got from Uncle Cuthbert! It's just like yours!" His teacher takes his hand and drags him through the doorway.

What in the world could Cuddy have that would be just like something of mine? What would I have that he would even want? He already has his own ornery grandmother, although he can certainly have mine. He has a mother, and he has his own bed. An annoying cousin? Is that what his uncle brought him? Because I should warn him not to accept that gift.

"How's your bread?" Mad Madge asks.

I scoop some with my spoon and smile at her while taking a bite. A spoonful of crumbs falls into my lap, but fortunately, Madge doesn't notice. Her interest is drawn to the magazine she's spread out on the table. She punches a page with her finger. "Aha! That's the ticket!" The headline jumps off the page: "How to Get Rich."

I nod as I skim the article over her shoulder.

HOW TO GET RICH.

Is there a mortgage on your property ? *Yes. I think. I'm not really sure what a mortgage is.*

Does your house need painting ?

Is new furniture wanted for the parlor ? *Yes.* *Yes. Inside and out.*

Would you like a college course next year ? *Absolutely not.*

Have you a good piano or organ ? *No. I don't have a bad piano or organ, either.*
Do you need stock or farming implements ?

Is there anything your heart desires that your pocket-book doesn't allow you to purchase ? *YES! First of all, I'm so*

IF THERE IS, YOU CAN HAVE IT.

There is a way to do everything. *I have been telling Granny this for years!*
There is a way to obtain honestly the necessary money for all your legitimate wants. *What about my not-so-legitimate wants?*

You don't know how ? We do.

(1.) We want to increase the subscription list of HOME AND COUNTRY MAGAZINE to **1,000,000 ;** and we are going to do it, for " where there is a will there is a way."

(2.) We need your help and are willing to pay liberally for it. *And I am willing to have you pay me! I like this already!*
This business will require from you neither previous experience nor the investment of capital.

We supply the capital and the ideas. *You* do the work and make the money. *I like the "money" part, but I'm not so sure about the "work" part.*
A fair question that will present itself to you is : **How much can I make ?** *I am thinking A LOT! A LOT of money!*

Divide the number of the population in your district by fifty ; multiply that by seventy-five, divide the product by one hundred, and it will give the amount *in dollars* that you can earn legitimately, honestly and agreeably within the next four weeks.

To learn how to do this will cost you only one penny. Think of it ! only one penny to send us your address and state that you want the latest and most reliable information about **How to Get Rich.**

HOME AND COUNTRY MAGAZINE,
This could be a problem. 53 East 10th Street, New York.

broke I don't even have a pocketbook. But after I get one of those, my heart

sword, a giant squid (for Cuddy), a pipe like Mr. Mulcrone's, some cowboy boots and spurs, a gun, a dress (NOT for me, obviously—for Mama!), a sheriff's badge . . .

desires a really sharp jackknife, a chess set, an ax, a yo-yo, a real

"I only need a penny!" Madge says. She looks at me, but I'm confused. How poor is she if she only needs a penny? Although, thinking about it, after giving Mama my weekly, hard-earned twenty-five cents, I don't have a penny, either. Which might mean I'm also poor.

But this isn't about me.

Madge stares at the magazine, a look of despair on her face. I know the feeling. I'm desperate to get rich, too. I have no idea why Madge needs money, but I'm sure she can't need it as much as I do.

Stanley Arthur Slater should not be sent to boarding school. And Stanley Arthur Slater's mama should not have to marry someone as evil as Archibald Crutchley. And Stanley Arthur Slater certainly should not have to claim such a person as his stepfather. For one thing, I already have a father. Granted, I may not have any idea where he is, but he's out there. And he's doing amazing things.

Like magic.

Or heroic things, like saving people from drowning.

Or making sure all the bad guys are locked up in jail.

And until he gets here, I need to hold down the fort. And the fort needs money, apparently.

"Hey!" Madge protests as I snatch the magazine from her grasp. I can't help it. I have to know how I can make some money and get Archibald Crutchley out of our hair for good. She grabs it back.

"Hey! I need that!" I say.

"Why do you need my magazine?" Mad Madge asks, holding it at arm's length from me.

"Why would I need it? Why would *you* need it, is a better question," I say, reaching for it. Mad Madge looks mad. I can see why she earned that nickname.

She peers at me. "You do realize no one calls me Mad Madge but you, right?"

I did not realize that.

"And that you're lucky I put up with it, because I would have pummeled most people into a mess of bones for calling me something other than my given name."

I just nod. I might be a tiny bit afraid of saying anything. I realize that sometimes I should probably keep my mouth shut.

"That's a fact," Madge says. "Also, not that it's any of your business, but I need money." Her attention drifts. "I want to travel the world, not end up stuck here like all the women in my family. I want to be like Nellie Bly."

Nellie Bly. Nellie Bly. I rack my brain. Never heard of her.

Mad Madge doesn't blink. "Why am I not surprised, Bedpan," she says. Her calm voice is soft and scary. "Nellie Bly, for your information, exposed asylum abuse and traveled the span of the entire earth in only seventy-two days. Does that ring a bell?"

Not another one. First Geri, with her highfalutin notion of becoming a doctor, and now Mad Madge. I thought she was smarter than that.

"Ah! Yes!" I respond as if I know what she's talking about. It is not a good idea to rile your personal bully—mine has a nasty temper and a goon of a cousin, and she's not afraid to use either one of them.

Madge rubs her nose and sniffs. "I'm going to get out of St. Ignace, Bedpan," she says. "See the world. There's got to be more than this." She waves a hand between us and around us. "I will never, ever, ever be poor if I can help it. No matter what it takes." She crumples up the magazine, tosses it under the table, and stomps off.

I finish my bread (without a spoon, because that's a ridiculous way to eat a piece of bread), throw the rest of my lunch in my mouth, and collect my pail. As I get up, I pick up the magazine. Maybe I can get rich, too. It doesn't ever hurt to gather information, and it's free! Which is a good sign, I think. It all seems so easy. Until I read this part, the part I didn't see earlier:

A fair question that will present itself to you is : **How much can I make?** *What does this even mean?*

Divide the number of the population in your district by fifty, multiply that by seventy-five, divide the product by one hundred, and it will give the amount *in dollars* that you can earn legitimately, honestly and agreeably within the next four weeks.

To learn how to do this will cost you only one penny. Think of it ! only one penny to send us your address and state that you want the latest and most reliable information about **How to Get Rich.**

Arithmetic. My sworn enemy.

Getting rich might be harder than it looks.

I'm not actually INSIDE the pickle.

CHAPTER 7

Now I am in a pickle.

"I'm hungry, Stan. Stan! I'm hungry," Cuddy moans, clutching his stomach dramatically.

"I know, Cuddy!" But I don't have any money because somewhere between lunch and now I lost the nickel Mrs. Carlisle gave me for Cuddy's snack, and I haven't quite figured out how to get around this problem. I drag Cuddy across the dusty street toward Chambers's Cigar Store. I hold my breath as I barrel in, Cuddy in tow. The hazy smoke makes it seem like everything has been half erased—it's all I can do to focus.

Cuddy coughs—his lungs can't tolerate smoke—so I

hurry and grab Mr. Carlisle's box of cigars before dragging Cuddy out. I don't want to lose him or else Mama and me will be up a creek without a paddle faster than you can say . . .

"Well, well, well, if it isn't Stan the Bedpan himself." It's Nincompoop.

"Look, Stan! Look! It's your friend Poopy Pants!" Cuddy says cheerily.

Nincompoop's eyes narrow. He throws the toothpick he had dangling from his lip onto the boardwalk.

"What did you call me?" he asks.

"Poopy—" I clamp a hand over Cuddy's mouth and think quick.

"Um. He didn't call you anything," I answer. "He said, 'Look at my goofy dance!'" I smile at Cuddy. "Go on! Show him your goofy dance, Cud! It's a good one," I assure Nincompoop.

"Huh? That's not what I said, Stan." Cuddy is not so good at embellishing the truth.

"You mean he's not so good at lying?" Nincompoop asks, stepping toward me.

"Great chat!" I grab Cuddy and pull him behind me like I'm a horse hauling an unwilling load.

LOADING LOGS, CHEBOYGAN, MICH.   Pub. by Sheble & Maxwell, New York, N. Y.

Nincompoop starts after us, but the James sisters cut him off at the corner and start asking him about his mother, and if there's one thing I've learned about that guy it's that he's much too polite for a career as a gangster.

"But! But!" Cuddy protests. "I'm still hungry! There's no food this way! And you know how I get when I'm hungry, Stan! I could faint." He groans, his body going limp. I'm simply trying to get us out of Nincompoop's sight before he follows us. I lug Cuddy quickly around the corner of the bank, right past the Dunham House, where Mrs. Campbell must be making some of her delicious apple pie. One whiff and I have a brilliant thought. I can take Cuddy to my house! Mama and Granny have been making cake all morning. Sure, it's for the boarders, but it will shut Cuddy up—and his never-satisfied stomach—and hopefully prevent him from telling his mother I didn't buy him anything to eat after school.

I am a genius. Plus, I'm hungry, too, and a piece of pound cake is just what the doctor ordered.

"What doctor, Stan? Are you taking me to the doctor? Because I do feel sick, Stan. Or hungry. I don't even know anymore," Cuddy wails.

"We're going to my house to get some cake, Cuddy! Doesn't that sound good?" I ask. As we get closer I remember Geri and how I have been commanded to be quiet. No, quieter than quiet. I have been told to be silent. As silent as a mouse. And Cuddy has never, ever been quiet. I'm pretty sure his favorite color is loud. I stop him at the walk leading to the door.

"Cuddy," I say, "my cousin Geri is in there. She is mean as a snake and ornery to boot, and she will probably run out of her room and punch you in the noggin if she hears you in the kitchen eating her pound cake." Cuddy's eyes grow larger than they usually are. "So we need to be quiet. Very, very quiet." Cuddy nods. I pat him on the head and nudge him toward the door.

"Come on in," I say. I drop the cigars on the table and usher Cuddy into the kitchen. A lovely golden-yellow pound cake is cooling for dinner.

A Narrow Escape from a Snake

"Hi, boys! Stan, is this Cuddy?" Mama asks, wiping her hands on her apron.

"Ma'am," Cuddy whispers with a slight smile. He hastily removes his cap and twists it in his hands.

Mama smiles back at him. If you didn't know Cuddy, you might think he's cute.

Oh, who am I kidding. He is kinda cute.

"Would you two like some pound cake?" Mama grabs the knife and cuts a couple of pieces. We pull up to the table and dig in.

"Thank you," Cuddy whispers.

"You are more than welcome," Mama whispers. "And you are always welcome in this home." She squeezes his shoulder.

We both inhale our cake.

"Now what, Stan? Now what?" Cuddy asks. Crumbs cling to his cheeks and sprinkle his mouth. I place a finger to my lips.

"Shhh!" I whisper.

He nods but starts kicking the table leg, which is definitely not an activity that will go unnoticed. I have to come up with more ideas to keep him quiet.

"Aha!" I have a great idea! "I'll be right back, Cud! Don't move!" I run upstairs, grab my scrapbook, and dash back down.

"Look what I have, Cuddy!" I place my most-prized possession on the kitchen table and open it. Cuddy sits on his hands and looks at the scrapbook like it's the Holy Grail.

Right then and there I realize he's never seen a scrapbook filled with pictures of far-off places and inventions, heroes and desperadoes. He's only seen the blank book I picked up at the post office.

"Where did you find all these pictures?" he whispers. "If there was a scrapbook prize, you would win first place." He looks at me. "There should be a scrapbook prize, Stan."

I appreciate his admiration. It *is* pretty special. And I agree. There should be a scrapbook prize.

For twenty-two and a half minutes, Cuddy doesn't move except to say, "Go to the next page, Stan. Can we go to the next page?" and I flip through, pointing out the outlaws and pirates, the ads for stockings and pictures of logging camps.

When it's time for me to take him home, Cuddy just sits at the table, speechless.

"Ready, my man?" I ask, holding open his coat. Cuddy stares at me as if a stiff wind blew in and froze him to the chair. "We have to get going, Cuddy, or your mom may worry." And your grandmother may hoist me by my breeches and hang me up like a porch swing.

"Stan, this has been the best day of my life," Cuddy says, plopping off the chair. He slides an arm into his sleeve and looks up at me. "Thank you for showing me your scrapbook, Stan. It's even better than I thought it would be."

I smile and help him with his other sleeve.

"You are my favorite person in the world, Stan. You are. And I want to be just like you when I get old."

I place his cap on his head, making sure it covers his ears.

"You're pretty great yourself. Now, let's get you home." And let's get out of here before our luck changes. We haven't seen Geri this whole time; I'm feeling pretty proud of my quiet, sneaky self. Also, I'm a whiz at taking care of Cuddy, I don't mind saying.

But as I grab the cigars off the table and we're halfway through the door, a voice stops us in our tracks—a voice thick and dark, as scratchy as a cat covered in sandpaper, and as scary as Granny holding a spoonful of cod liver oil.

Even scratchier than this!

Even scarier than that!

"Where are you going?" the voice asks. Cuddy has a look of horror on his face. His eyes widen, and his mouth drops open. He knots his fingers through mine.

There on the sofa sits Geri. The kerosene lamp casts a shadow over her and the gargantuan book propped on her lap. Her skin is so transparent it almost glows. "I'll be right back," I tell her, and herd Cuddy out the door before he thinks my home is inhabited by a creepy, sinister ghost.

THE GHOST. – A CHRISTMAS FROLIC.   LE REVENANT.

"What was that?" Cuddy asks. He stumbles along like an old man who's lost his memory.

"That was nothing," I answer, hoping Cuddy will soon forget this experience. I'm also trying to come up with an acceptable story I can tell his mother when he comes home with that spooked look on his face.

Should I mention Cuddy's overactive imagination? His inability to tell fact from fiction? His impulsiveness?

"That certainly wasn't nothing," Cuddy replies.

"Yes, yes, it was!" I insist. I wave to Mr. Mulcrone clopping down the street in his fancy new carriage with the lights on the sides.

HARPER'S MAGAZINE ADVERTISER.

DESIGN is what makes the Carriage; for it represents the thought that is put into it. In planning our Select Carriages we have corralled all that the experience of over thirty years could suggest, skill devise, and taste approve. The marked ingless architecture, ous in many models, the admiration of every vehicle. No finer prourious appointments, ethics of fine Carriage divergence from mean which is so conspicu will readily command lover of a distinctive ductions, no more luxno greater study in the building exist to-day.

You don't get much fancier than this.—

A VISIT OR CORRESPONDENCE INVITED.

THE FRENCH CARRIAGE CO.,

FERDINAND F. FRENCH.

Builders and Designers of Selected Carriages,

83–85 Summer Street, - - - BOSTON, MASS.

"How can you say that?" Cuddy stops and confronts me. I take a deep breath. Apparently I won't be able to make him forget such a frightful sight so easily.

"Cuddy, what you saw in there was scary, I'll admit," I admit.

"Scary, Stan? Scary?" Cuddy practically yells. This is worse than I thought.

"I know! I know! But it's really not as bad as you think," I insist. "I promise! She's not usually so frightening!"

Well, that's a lie. She's *always* frightening. But if it will calm Cuddy down, I'll say anything at this point.

"Frightening, Stan? Frightening?" Cuddy yells.

I panic and clutch Cuddy's arms, forcing him to look at me. "What do you think about what you just saw?" I ask.

Cuddy lets out a sigh. "Only that I just laid eyes on the most beautiful creature God ever put on this earth," he says.

You have got to be kidding.

Cuddy is in love with Geri.

*At this point
I might as well
just
<u>be</u>
a pickle.*

CHAPTER 8

I am now so much in a pickle I smell like dill, my face is green, and I have little bumps all over me.

Either that, or I dropped a jar of them, feel like throwing up, and am breaking out in hives simply thinking about the mess I'm in.

I didn't dare walk Cuddy in—I just dropped him off at the door and skedaddled.

"I want to show you what my uncle got me, Stan," Cuddy pleaded. But I certainly couldn't afford to run into Mrs. Carlisle. What if she asked about the nickel I lost? If she found out about the nickel, it's very possible I would lose my job watching Cuddy.

I winked at Cuddy and promised I would see his surprise soon, when we had more time. Then I called him Champ, which always makes him happy, and dashed back home before anyone could stop and question me.

But the truth is, I'm worried. I don't have a job like Archibald Crutchley—I can't earn enough as a child minder to keep Mama from marrying that guy if money becomes an issue. My quarter dollar is a drop in the bucket, though you wouldn't know it when I hand it over to Mama—she smiles at me like I've given her the moon and everything is going to be okay.

Everything will *not* be okay, however, if Mrs. Carlisle finds out about that nickel—I need to pay her back, and I'm afraid that's not possible.

I need a plan. A plan to get rich. And a way to do it quickly. I pull Mad Madge's magazine from my pocket and smooth it out on my bed. It's from New York City, a place where people make their millions every single day. I'm pretty sure. There must be something in here for me. Something that doesn't require math.

I flip past an article about politicians and a picture of Washington Hesing and his whiskers, past all the ads for shoes and pianos.

Also, I wish Geri would stop her hacking; it's making it difficult to concentrate.

WASHINGTON HESING,
As He Appeared Before the Wind Blew Through His Whiskers.

After

There's nothing in these pages that will help me solve my problem today. Betting on the Kentucky Derby wouldn't bring any kind of reward until May, a whole month away, even if I did have money to place a bet.

I'm ready to toss the magazine on the floor in disgust when I see something that won't help me but certainly might help Geri.

It's not in my character to help someone so devious and disagreeable, but if it will stop her cough, I'm willing to try it.

It's an ad for a remedy so amazing it promises to cure colds, catarrh (whatever that is), and nervous disease (whatever that is), and it will make you smarter. Which Geri certainly could use. I run to show Mama. I think I've found a cure for what ails Geri!

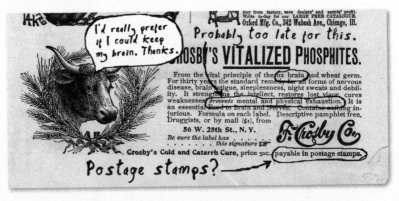

"Mama! Look!" I holler, careening down the stairs and into the kitchen. But when I turn the corner, I'm met with a hand to the chest that nearly knocks me back to next week.

"Oof!" I can barely catch my breath.

"Stanley Arthur Slater," Granny hisses. "You will hush

up immediately. This is a boardinghouse, a place where businessmen pay good money to live, and they certainly won't stay here if they are constantly disturbed by a boy who cannot control his impulses!" She nods toward Mr. Glashaw napping in his chair. That old coot couldn't hear an explosion if it went off next to his head.

"But, Granny!" I yell. She glares. "Um, but, Granny?" I say in my church voice.

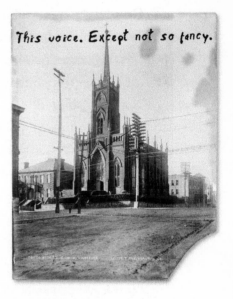

This voice. Except not so fancy.

"I found a cure for Geri!" I thrust the magazine at her. Granny takes the wrinkly paper in two fingers.

"Right here! Right where it says 'Crosby's Vitalized Phosphites.' See it? Look! The 'vitalized' is even underlined! See where it cures everything? We should order it! We should order it right now!" I poke the paper for emphasis.

Granny smiles. It's a sad smile. A smile that basically says, "Oh, you poor, ignorant child."

"No, that's not my smile that said that, Stan. That was my mouth."

Oh.

"And this is simply snake oil, Stan."

"Nope. It's ox brain. See? It says it right here!" I point to where I've circled "ox brain." That seems important.

And disgusting. "I don't care what it's made of, Granny. If it works, it could be snake poo and I'd make Geri take it."

Granny looks like she's smelled snake poo.

"Can we order it? Can we?"

"Stan, snake oil isn't from a snake; it's simply a term for something a salesman tries to pass off as a cure-all, when it might end up being a vial of water and lemon or turpentine or mineral oil. It doesn't actually help; it takes money from good, hardworking people, creates hope, and leaves folks in despair. It's a scam." She hands the magazine back to me.

I am disappointed.

"Come to think of it, that's how Eugene made his fortune," Granny says, looking toward the backyard as if she can see him through the walls.

Eugene "Genius" Malone?

I'm instantly interested, because if I can cure Geri *and* make money, that's a situation where everybody wins!

"How, Granny? How did Eugene Malone make his fortune?"

"As I remember, he went out West and then came back and sold questionable medical remedies at medicine shows. Made a ton of money."

This is all I need to hear. If Eugene can do it, I can, too. I've met that guy and, no offense, he's not a genius.

But my plan is, if I do say so myself. And it's so clever, it just might save Mama and me from a fate worse than death: a future with Mr. Crutchley.

All I need is a recipe, a willing patient, and some bottles, and we'll be rich! I'm off to start my new business venture!

"It's also the reason Eugene almost ended up in prison," Granny says as I head up the stairs.

But that's not important. No one puts rich people in prison. Also, my medicine will work.

I can practically count the money already.

After dinner I throw scraps outside for the cats. Granny loves them. She's even named all of them. There's Billy. And the white one with a limp is called Billy. And the big one that always meows the loudest is named Billy. Actually, they're all named Billy. Granny has never been

And another Billy
(even though it's a girl).

And Billy.

Billy

And Freckles.
Just kidding.
It's Billy.

Look, it's Billy!

known for her keen imagination, which might just be why she doesn't appreciate mine.

"Clem!" I hear from near the tracks. "Clem!"

I sigh. "It's Stan, Eugene. S-t-a-n."

"Yep. That's what I said." Eugene meanders over, all grime and matted hair. "What's the news on the streets? I see old Archie's been over quite often." Eugene winks at me like he knows something I don't.

He must know something I don't.

"Do you know something I don't, Eugene?"

"Well, Clem, I know that Archibald Crutchley is a bit of a namby-pamby who is sweet on your mama."

That's common knowledge. Once again, I'm thinking Eugene's nickname of "Genius" is wishful thinking on someone's part.

"And I know he's got money. When I had money, I was much more attractive to the ladies, if you know what I mean." He winks again.

I do not know what he means. But I do know he used to be rich. And he used to be rich because he sold "medicine." And I need money. Some might say I'm desperate for money.

"Well, I certainly know that feeling," Eugene says, drawing a hand through his hair and slapping his cap back on his head. "I have to say, not having any money is somewhat more freeing than having a lot of money."

"Pfft," I scoff, waving a hand at him. What kind of nonsense is this?

"No, really, Clem! I've got nothing to lose!" He spits and rubs it into the dirt with his shoe.

Suddenly I have an idea. "Eugene," I say slyly. I reach down for a daisy and start picking off the petals, pretending to be completely caught up in this meaningless activity.

"She loves you, she loves you not," Eugene says with each petal I toss to the ground.

"Huh?" I ask, confused.

I sure hope she loves me not.

"Who are you sweet on, eh, Clem? You can tell me! We're just guys on the stoop shooting the breeze, you and I." He sits on the step next to me, cats weaving themselves through his legs as he pets them. "Hey, Billy," Eugene purrs.

I have a pang of sudden guilt. I just gave a plate of good food scraps to a bunch of cats when we have a hungry man living a few feet from us. Why didn't I give the plate to him?

Eugene claps a hand on my shoulder. "I'm set, Clem. Don't you worry about me. Anyway, you seemed like you were about to ask me something. Women problems? I'm kind of an expert on women, if I do say so myself. Speaking of which, how's that Granny of yours?" Eugene winks at me again.

I pretend I don't hear that last part. "Um, anyway, I was

thinking about medicine, Eugene." I'm actually thinking about how to avoid boarding school, but one thing at a time.

"Boarding school's not all that bad," Eugene says. A cat perches on his shoulder, and three more lie at his feet. "It was great for me. Intellectually stimulating, some great guys. I wouldn't rule it out."

I'm really starting to question this guy's mental capacity. "Um, anyway, Eugene, what I was wondering is, my cousin Geri is very sick and I heard through the grapevine that you know a thing or two about medical cures." I scratch circles in the dirt with a stick.

"True, true. The key is actual snake oil; it really does have curative properties, but it's quite hard to get, especially here in Michigan. I used to buy it from Chinese railroad workers when I was out West."

"Can I get some of that oil, Eugene? Do you have the address of any of those Chinese railroad workers? It's kind of urgent." I am on a deadline here, mister.

Eugene shakes his head slowly so as not to knock Billy off his perch on his shoulder. "Nope. Sorry, Clem."

He has called me Clem so many times now, I'm starting to answer to it. "Why not?"

Eugene leans back on his hands, the cats adjusting themselves accord-

How hard can it really be to oil one of these things?

ingly. "I don't have those connections anymore, see. Also, you don't want to be selling snake oil treatments. It's a business that preys on people's hopes and dreams, and the money you make at the expense of other people is certainly not worth it."

"But what if it works? Then isn't it worth it?"

"Well, without the actual snake oil, chances are it won't work. . . ."

"But what if it does?"

"I guarantee today's snake oil medicines are fraudulent. Why, they add turpentine. . . ."

"The stuff that takes off paint?" Turpentine is nastier than a flea on a flea on a tick.

"Yessir. I think Hamlin's Wizard Oil has some ammonia in it, too. And alcohol."

I shudder. It sounds nasty. But then I remember I won't be taking it. Geri will! So the nastier, the better!

"What else?" I ask eagerly. I'm listing all the ingredients in my head so I can rummage through the cupboards later and create my first batch of Stanley Slater's Incredible Cure-All! A doctor in a bottle! I imagine all the money I'll make. How we'll fix the roof on the boardinghouse, along with the fence and the front porch. Then we'll buy new furniture for the parlor and hang some curtains. . . .

"And that's about it," Eugene says, gently shooing cats from his lap as he gets up.

"What's about it?" Did I miss the last few ingredients? Wait!

"See you around, Clem." Eugene smiles. His teeth are amazingly white, gleaming from his grimy face.

"But I missed some of the ingredients!" I say. Eugene apparently doesn't hear me, however, as he whistles his way down the tracks, probably on his way to Reverend Elliot's.

I suppose I can make some of this up. It can't be that hard. I try to think of the most disgusting things I can possibly come up with because medicine always tastes terrible, so something awful has got to work really well.

I run up to my room, pull out my scrapbook and some magazines, and start brainstorming the worst-tasting ingredients possible.

1. Turpentine — get from Granny. When she's not looking.

2. Ammonia — get from cleaning supplies. When no one is looking.

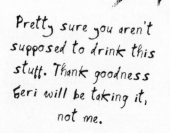

[PATENTED NOV. 26, 1878.]

C. C. PARSONS'
Household ☙ Ammonia
TRADE MARK.
QUARTS. PINTS. HALF-PINTS.
WHAT IT WILL DO.

It will absolutely deodorize and cleanse Sinks, Closets, Baths, Utensils and Clothes, in the Nursery, Sick Rooms, and Household generally.

It will clean Paint, Marble, Glass, etc., instantly, leaving a light gloss.

It is unequaled in cleansing the finest Lace without injury.

It will freshen Dress Goods, Furniture Coverings and Carpets, etc., removing all grease and stains.

It will clean Brushes and Combs as if by Magic.

It will, in the laundry, clean perfectly without injuring the most delicate colors or fabric.

It will instantly kill Bedbugs and other Insects.

It is the most delightful article for the toilet ever known or used, removing all odor, and will keep the skin smooth, soft and white.

Clear Ammonia and all imitations are nothing but FREE ALKALI, and are ruinous to clothes and irritating to the skin, making it rough, red and sore; They are made to deceive the public, and should not be allowed in the Family or Household.

Insist on having C. C. PARSONS' HOUSEHOLD AMMONIA.

Sole Manufacturers and Proprietors,
Columbia Chemical Works,
21, 23, 25, 27, 29 AND 31 JAY STREET,
BROOKLYN, N. Y.

Pretty sure you aren't supposed to drink this stuff. Thank goodness Geri will be taking it, not me.

Here's where it gets tricky.

3. Soap—not that I've ever really tasted it. For using bad language or anything.

4. Onions—enough said.

5. Cat fur—maybe I licked a cat once. It was an accident.

6. Licorice—only an adult would call this candy.

7. Earwax—again, not that I've ever really tasted it. Or, if I did, it was an accident.

8. Cigar butts—that was an accident, too. It's amazing how much they look like candy when it's dark.

9. Worms—I'm just now realizing all the awful things I've accidentally tasted.

Not nearly as tasty as you might think. Too many worms and not enough cake. →

I set down my pen. Would I really make Geri take this? And, even if I could, why would I give it to innocent people who have never done anything to me?

This is one of those moral dilemmas my teacher, Miss Wenzel, is always talking about, one of those times when you have to make a choice but you don't really like either option.

Moral dilemmas make my head spin, but I can't help wondering if I'm doing the right thing. I could make bucket-loads of money from my new snake oil invention and solve all our problems. But if the medicine doesn't work, people will spend their own hard-earned money on something that doesn't actually cure anything.

The other option is to do nothing, and if I do that, Mama becomes Alice Crutchley, I refuse to become Stan Crutchley, I am sent to live at a boarding school where I'm forced to wear a tie and clean pants and end up dying of boredom and unbearable cleanliness. Then Mama and Mr. Crutchley have lots of Crutchley babies (all of them with names start-

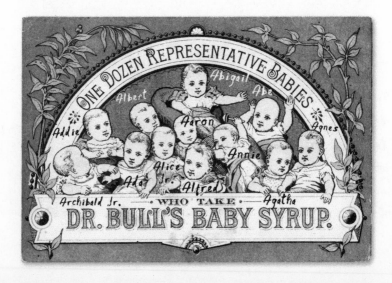

ing with the letter A) and my poor grave will be forgotten and overgrown with weeds.

So my moral dilemma seems to be cheating people or dying of boredom. And I just can't decide which option is worse.

I turn off my kerosene lamp, tuck myself into bed, and stare at the ceiling. Moonlight bounces off the dresser mirror. I wish my life were easier. I wish my life were like Cuddy's, a guy whose biggest concern is whether or not his uncle actually saw a mermaid off the coast of Canada.

When I finally fall asleep, I dream about mermaids and turpentine and Archibald Crutchley and Canada, and when I wake up, it's clear: Mermaids scare me, weird things happen in Canada, and turpentine surely isn't as bad as it's made out to be.

Also, Archibald Crutchley must be stopped.

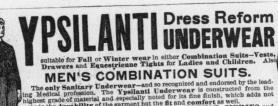

I'd say Granny's underwear drawer is probably the best place to hide something. Because I won't be going in there. Ever.

CHAPTER 9

Mama says, "Absolutely not," when she spies me with the turpentine. Then she grabs it and hides it somewhere I will never look. Like Granny's underwear drawer. So I'm left on my own to come up with something awful.

- *One tablespoon of vinegar*

- *One forkful of dirt*

- *One teaspoon of oil*

- 4 pinches of salt

- Mr. Glashaw's cigar ashes

Stir violently with a spoon. Clean up mess with a rag. But not a white rag, because then Granny will know you're up to something.

"I am not drinking that. It smells like cat vomit," Geri says forcefully.

"But it will cure what ails you!" I insist. Does she want to get better or not?

"Not if I have to drink that!"

I dump my magic concoction out the front door, where it melts into the mud.

Granny says, "Are you insane, child?" when she spies me with the ammonia. "That stuff will make you blind!" Then she hides it somewhere I will never look. Like her underwear drawer. So I'm left on my own, again, to come up with something even more awful.

- One tablespoon of mud

- 4 slivers of soap

- One can of Beardsley's Shredded Codfish

- Sarsaparilla

- One teaspoon of cod liver oil

Stir gently with a fork. Try not to spill onto Granny's freshly ironed white tablecloth. Cover stain on tablecloth with a napkin. Place kerosene lamp on napkin. Pray Granny doesn't notice.

"I am not drinking that! It looks like the tub after Granny gets done with her bath, and it smells like Tucker Lester's fish market!" Geri peers at it with a scowl. "What did you put in there? Soap? Who eats soap?"

Who eats soap, indeed. Why, perhaps curious, imaginative people eat soap.

It was only once, and I wouldn't recommend it.

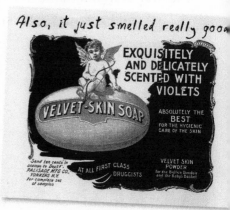

Also, it just smelled really good

I dump my ingenious potion out the back door. One of the Billys sniffs it and starts hacking up a hair ball.

- One hair ball, preferably fresh

- 4 teaspoons of sugar

- The rest of whatever was in the bottle I found out back by the railroad tracks

- The last pickled pig's foot, chopped

- Vegetable glycerin (vegetables are good for you!)

Don't even try mixing it together. But do try not to spill it on the napkin under the kerosene lamp that is covering the stain on Granny's white tablecloth. Remove the kerosene lamp, cover the old napkin with a new napkin, and replace the lamp.

"Stan, you can't be serious. Who would ever ingest something that looks like you've scraped it off the bottom of your shoe? Plus, it smells like Eugene Malone on a bad day." Geri's nose wrinkles in disgust.

"I'm trying to cure you, Geri! I'm spending all my

precious time trying to come up with a cure for whatever it is that ails you!" I wave my cure in the air for emphasis. Geri jumps like I might spill some on her.

As if I would ever spill anything.

"I appreciate your concern," she sighs, "but I'm almost positive I simply have influenza and there's nothing we can do medically to cure it. A mustard plaster . . ."

Mustard! I should have used mustard! It tastes bad and smells bad and would be perfect in my next cure-all!

How did I forget about mustard?

"Are you even listening to me?" Geri's voice is soft but firm. It makes me think she's feeling better, but then her chest heaves and her gasp of breath reminds me of a stick scraping up a washboard.

Granny bustles in and thumps Geri on the back so hard I think she might knock out some teeth.

If we're lucky, she'll knock some sense into her.

"Now is not the time for your silly jokes, Stanley. Go fetch some water," Granny commands.

Fortunately, she has not noticed the jar of hair-bally pig's-foot oil I'm holding. It really is disgusting. I drop the entire thing into the trash and pour Geri a glass of water.

I wonder if I should add something to it. Maybe some alcohol? I haven't tried that yet. Or what about some kerosene? That's got to taste awful.

"Stanley! What on earth is taking you so long?" Granny yells.

I hustle back with the water. My entrepreneurial spirit is squashed in this place and not at all appreciated in this family.

But when I see Geri bent over, Granny's forehead grooved with worry, I have to admit I feel sad for her. And I wonder about me.

Do I really want to earn my fortune from the suffering of others?

And how do I make sure to avoid my own suffering?

My good friend Stinky Pete always says that life is a series of choices. And if I have a say in the matter, my choices aren't going to include boarding school or a Mr. Archibald Crutchley.

Unfortunately, I don't usually have a say in the matter.

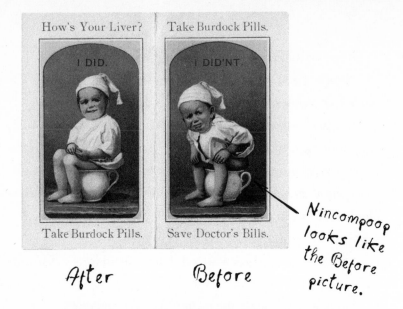

How's Your Liver? | Take Burdock Pills.

I DID. | I DID'NT.

Take Burdock Pills. | Save Doctor's Bills.

After   Before

Nincompoop looks like the Before picture.

CHAPTER 10

Mondays are the worst. There's school, of course. Even though the school year is nearing its end, Mama and Granny still make me go. As if I'm going to learn anything I don't already know in these last few weeks. It's a well-known fact the most important things in life can't be learned in school. Such as:

1. Run away from bullies. Especially girl bullies. And especially if you've accidentally said their much larger cousin looks like the "before" picture for a medical cure. And if the cousin accidentally hears you say that.

B. Don't engage seven-year-old boys in conversation. Unless you want to hear nonstop talking about optical illusions or how beautiful your cousin Geri is for the rest of your life. Or at least until you pull out your scrapbook. Come to think of it, believing Geri is beautiful is an optical illusion. It's all making sense now.

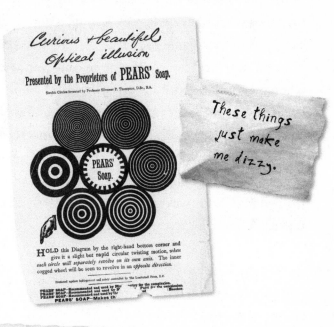

These things just make me dizzy.

3rd. Money is the root of all evil. Unless you want to buy something. Or make sure your mama isn't forced to marry someone just because money is an issue.

Finally, being a whiz at most things doesn't mean you can easily make money. Although it definitely should mean that.

These are the times in my life when I wish I had a dad around. And by "dad" I mean my dad. The one I've never met. Who obviously doesn't know of my existence or he never would have left. But I could also mean a guy like Stinky Pete, my dangerous friend from the lumber camp. The one who said he would stop in and visit Mama and me when he got done with the river drive. The one who taught me it's never too late to be what you might have been.

I've never been rich, and I sure hope it's not too late for that.

Cuddy waves a picture in my face. "Can you see it, Stan? Can you see the optical illusion? Can you see both things? Can you?" Cuddy waves the picture so wildly I can't see anything but blurs.

All I can see is a furry dog wearing a bug as a hat.

MY WIFE AND MY MOTHER-IN-LAW
They are both in this picture — Find them

"Hold on! Let me look at it more closely."

"Now see what it says, Stan? See! There's a wife and a mother-in-law in the picture!" Cuddy points to the bottom of the page, but I'm not a fellow who reads the fine print. I'm a lone wolf, making my way through the world by himself. Quietly. Like a spy. Never even recognized.

"Hey, Stan!" Mr. France waves hello.

Sneaky. So unnoticeable, I'm practically a ghost.

"How ya doing, Stan?" Mr. Standish tips his cap my way.

A man winding his way through life and the wild, a stranger in a strange land. Exploring roads never before traveled.

"Stanley." Martha Standish bats her eyelashes at me as she steps off the curb. I lend her a hand. "Nice seeing you at church on Sunday."

I nod and return a smile. Now. Where was I?

"For someone so lonely, you sure know a lot of people, Stan," Cuddy says.

"And he's quite the ladies' man, it appears," a gruff voice says from behind me. I know that voice! I swing around to see the bearded, ruddy face of Stinky Pete, cold-blooded killer.

I can't help myself. I fling my arms around him like he's the last branch on a tall, tall tree and a grizzly bear waits for me at the bottom.

Stinky Pete hoots and wraps his solid arms around me.

If I were a girl, I probably would have cried when I saw that guy. But I'm not a girl, no matter what Nincompoop says. And even though Stinky Pete's coat looks like something wet might have landed on it in the general area where my eyes were, I did not cry on his jacket.

It was probably wet before I even hugged him.

I wipe my eyes as Stinky Pete grabs me.

"Let me take a look at you! I think you've grown three feet in the past month! You're becoming quite the man," he says with a grin.

He always knows just what to say. And, in this case, it's the truth.

"Oh, he's not a man, sir. He's only eleven. And he's not even as tall as my mother," Cuddy says.

"And who do we have here, Stan? A new friend?" Stinky Pete wraps his arm around me in a manly kind of way. I had forgotten about Cuddy for a moment.

"Cuthbert Carlisle the Third, sir," Cuddy says, thrusting out a hand. "But you can call me Cuddy."

"Well, nice to make your acquaintance, Cuddy," Stinky Pete says, wrapping Cuddy's pudgy hand in both of his.

"I'm Stan's best friend," Cuddy says.

My best friend, I realize, is a seven-year-old.

"And I will be marrying his cousin Geri in a few years, so then we'll be related, too!" Cuddy jumps up and down with excitement. It's the first I've heard of this plan.

"Sounds like you've got it all figured out," Stinky Pete says, his eyes all a-twinkle.

When he turns back toward me, I instantly remember how old my other best friend is. . . .

I don't actually know how old Stinky Pete is, but I do know he's my other best friend.

"What are you doing here, Stinky Pete? Have you seen Mama? Just to warn you, Granny and Geri are at the house, too." I feel it's necessary to let him know.

"I figured. Geri was pretty sick at camp. She feeling better?" Stinky Pete asks.

"She's beautiful," Cuddy says, looking wistfully off in the distance.

Stinky Pete laughs. "Oh, I know that feeling, Cuddy, my boy." He punches his arm gently.

I shrug. "I'm trying to cure her and make a lot of money in the process, but I'm not having any luck," I say. Although she does seem to be feeling better, despite the fact that she hasn't even taken a sip of my cures.

"Luck has very little to do with making money, Stan. There's no substitute for hard work," Stinky Pete says seriously.

"Yeah, well, what about Cuddy's uncle who went to Alaska and tripped on some gold lying on the ground and next thing you know, he's rich?" I ask.

"I'm pretty sure there's more to that story," Stinky Pete says.

"No," Cuddy says. "That's exactly what happened. And then someone

A little luck certainly wouldn't hurt.

Also, I might need a new pair of pants.

ITS LUCKY HE'S GOT THOSE
WAIST BANDS ON THEY'LL
STAND THE STRAIN.

STARK'S UNIQUE WAIST BAND

stole all of Uncle Cuthbert's fortune and Father had to wire him a lot of money so he could buy a railroad ticket home."

"Hmmm. I see," Stinky Pete says.

"And then he made a lot of money selling soap," Cuddy adds.

I look at him like he's grown a third ear on top of his noggin. "Soap, Cuddy? Like the stuff we just picked up for your mother?"

Cuddy nods his head so hard, if he actually did have a third ear, it would have flown off and landed in the street.

"How does someone make money selling soap?" Also, I might need to know this.

Stinky Pete doesn't look surprised. "Was he out in Colorado?"

"Yep! See, Stan! I told you!" Cuddy punches a finger my way. "Mr. Pete has heard of it!"

"Have you?" I ask.

He nods. "Sure have." He looks over at Cuddy and adds, "Wouldn't be my choice for how to earn an honest dollar, but I can tell you more about that at dinner."

"And you'll tell me how I can make my fortune selling soap?" I ask. How dishonest can it be? It's soap!

"And then we'll talk about the best ways to make money," Stinky Pete agrees.

"I don't have to make any money," Cuddy says. "Father has lots of it. Although he says if Mother's good-for-nothing brother doesn't stop asking for money, we'll end up in the poorhouse."

But I'm not really listening. I'm looking at the ground, hoping to trip on gold. And coming up with a soap recipe that will make me rich.

I've already figured out one ingredient, and that would be soap.

Stinky Pete grins and says again how glad he is to see me.

"Are you leaving? You're not leaving, are you?" I'm trying not to sound desperate, but truth be told, I'm desperate.

"I'm leaving for now. Got to get back to work. Money doesn't grow on trees," he says with a wink. "I'll see you at dinner, though!"

Stinky Pete tips his cap to Cuddy and me and whistles his way down the street.

"Do you need money, Stan?" Cuddy asks. He looks as concerned as a seven-year-old can, and I decide, as the mature one in this relationship, not to worry him over my problems.

"Nah, Cuddy. I'm fine. We're fine," I reassure him.

But I must not have sounded very convincing, because as we head toward the mercantile to pick up some things for Mrs. Carlisle, he says, "Because there's always organized crime, Stan. That's one way to make some money. And fast."

I quickly brake on my heels. What does Cuddy know about organized crime?

Also, I might not be a whiz at being organized.

"I know a lot about a lot of things, Stan. And I keep all that information in my—"

"But," I interrupt, "what do you know about organized crime and making a fast dollar?"

"Well," Cuddy replies, "I would not recommend a life of organized crime, but if you're interested . . ." His eyes spark like a match when first lit.

Like this. But brighter.

Not that I would know, since I don't play with matches. Except for the one time I lit my eyebrows on fire.

But I don't want to talk about that.

"So, Stan, organized crime in this country started in New York. Do you know where New York is, Stan?" I nod. "The Forty Thieves made up one gang. My uncle helped form them. He's really dangerous." I steer Cuddy away from the group of businessmen smoking cigars and chatting on the corner. Cuddy's voice is loud, and if I'm going to start a life of crime because I have no other choice, I don't need people to know about it.

I'm not saying this is a good idea, but . . .

"Then some Italians formed the Mafia and started stealing things and then selling them. That's one way of making fast money, Stan!" Cuddy looks excited.

I'm worried, however. First of all, why is Cuddy so excited about stealing things? And, two, I don't feel very good about stealing. Even if we do need money, I'm almost positive that's not the way to make it.

"Oh, I'm not saying it's a good idea. In fact, I think it's a bad idea. Unless you want to end up going to prison. And prison is not a very nice place, Stan."

Famous Adventures and Prison Escapes of the Civil War

300 PAGES

FULLY ILLUSTRATED

PRICE $2.00

I'll end up having to do this.

PASSING THE OUTER WALL

Published by THE CENTURY CO.

Cuddy kicks a stone down the road into the path of an oncoming buggy. I pull him back before he runs into the street after it.

I saved his life. I wish someone would pay me every time I had to do that. I'd be a millionaire.

Cuddy keeps talking as we weave through town, stopping to get a shaving stick and toilet soap, some other things I've already forgotten. I hurry him out of Steinberg's when the phone rings. I cannot be seen with a corset on my arm again and continue to call myself a man.

"You're not a man," Cuddy kindly reminds me. I don't even have time to stick up for myself before he starts carrying on again. About organized crime and Boss Tweed.

And his uncle who sold gold bricks that weren't really gold but that people bought anyway.

Boss—y Tweed reminds me of someone.

How can someone sell gold bricks if they aren't actually gold?

And how can they do it without getting caught?

"Oh, they all get caught, Stan." Cuddy's sticky again from the gumdrops Mr. Steinberg gave him. I should be paying closer attention. I haul him down by the dock as he chatters on and on, wet my shirtsleeve, toss his gumdrops into the sand, and wipe his face.

Don't think I don't realize for a minute that this is exactly something Granny would do to me.

"Hey! I wasn't done with those!" Cuddy complains. I rub his face to get all the sticky off.

"Yeah, well, we'll get you more tomorrow. We've got to get you somewhat cleaned up before I take you home, or your grandmother will never let me near you again."

Cuddy's eyes brim with tears, but he doesn't argue. "We can't have that happen, Stan! You're my best friend!"

I dry his face as best I can with my other sleeve, pick up the packages I've set on the dock, and point Cuddy toward the hill leading to his house.

"We'll be okay," I assure him. "We'll be fine." This time I think I'm trying to reassure myself.

"Can you come in today and see what my uncle got me? Huh, Stan? Can you?"

I shake my head. "Sorry, Cud. I've got to get home for dinner. Maybe tomorrow?" I add. Stinky Pete will be at dinner and will hopefully have some get-rich-quick ideas for me. He did say he'd tell me the secret for making money.

"It's like yours!" Cuddy says. I have no idea what he's talking about because I've got other things on my mind. Major things. Things manly men think about, like organized crime and gold and soap, a miracle cure for whatever ails you, and bacon, because I can't ever stop thinking about bacon. Even while I'm eating it.

This is exactly how I feel about bacon.

CHAPTER 11

Nothing worth having comes easy, Stan." Stinky Pete acts like he's talking to me, but he's gazing at Mama, a lopsided grin on his face.

Mama holds out a bowl of baked beans, a dreamy smile on her lips. Baked beans do that to some people. Granny glares at both of them, her arms crossed.

"I saw Archibald today. In a new carriage. He seems to be doing very well financially," Granny says, her voice as clipped as Cuddy's hair after a trip to the barber.

It can't be easy to cut hair on a Ferris wheel, but it's probably a lot more fun.

But no one is listening to her.

"I hear you have a job, Stan," Stinky Pete says. "Your mother says you've been working hard, taking care of Cuddy and contributing to the family piggy bank. That's got to feel good, right?" He looks at me while sopping up some baked beans with the bread heel.

You know, it does feel good. I sit up a little straighter. And I'm pretty good at that job, I realize. That also feels good.

Geri coughs from the other room. She finally got out of bed for a little while today. At least long enough to tell me I had dark circles under my eyes and looked like I might be coming down with something. That's how I knew she was feeling better.

But I've been worried I'm dying ever since.

Then she ate some soup and went right back to bed.

I peeked in to look at her. I told her she looked so bad she'd better not go outside or the dogcatcher might pick her up.

But she didn't even reply. So then I felt really bad, which is not a feeling I'm all too familiar with, especially concerning Geri. So I brought her a magazine. One that didn't even have much cut out of it. And I read her a story about artistic house furnishing and then one about the art of knitting and then started on about misses' and girls' fashions until she growled at me that she didn't want to be a seamstress, she wanted to be a doctor.

"A doctor, Stan!" she said so strongly I'm pretty sure it sapped her of a week's worth of energy.

I didn't have the heart to remind her she's a girl and girls are better suited to doing girlie things, like sewing. Instead, I read her a story called "Love on Leaden Wings" until she fell asleep. Or until I fell asleep.

I might have fallen asleep.

I don't know why girls like this stuff so much.

LOVE ON LEADEN WINGS.

I fell asleep right about here.

BY ERNEST C. WHITTON.

IN the puritanical days of the seventeenth century, when Bristol was the leading seaport of England, and its good people went to church regularly on Sunday, and just as regularly dealt in African slaves on Monday, there lived in a narrow street behind the old church (in the house of William Watts, tinman, pewterer and slater), a man who had formerly been a large hosier of London, and who by no means shared the opinion of the Bristol merchants as to the legitimacy of slave commerce. As hosier, Daniel Defoe had failed for a large sum and escaped to Bristol, but even here he was not let alone. The Bristol slave-dealers, becoming incensed at his avowed antagonism to their most profitable commerce, informed his London creditors, who charged the local constables to arrest him and bring him to prison for debt. This persecution obliged him to take advantage of the old British maxim in law, "An Englishman's home is his castle," * and remain locked in his room from Monday morning till Saturday night to be free from arrest. For, according to law, no one could open or cause to be opened a locked door to arrest a man for debt.

So it was that the good people of Bristol only saw the fugitive London merchant on Sunday when no man could be arrested for debt. On these days he always appeared faultlessly dressed, with a rapier hanging at his side, and in spite of the enmity he had incurred his manly bearing and dignified appearance, coupled with the fact that he was known to have fought for his opinions with sword and pen, won admiration from all. This was Daniel Defoe at thirty.

One beautiful Sunday morning in September, 1692, while the church-bells were ringing out their merry chimes calling the pious people to morning service, the sun sent its grateful rays into the small room where sat the man whose name was destined to go down to posterity—whose praises would be sung at every fireside for generations to come—the author of "Robinson Crusoe." He was in deep reflection for a suitable title to his newest work, in which he expressed his opinions about national economy. The manuscript lay before him on the table, a silent witness of his unceasing work, his hours of thought, and his undaunted determination. As he sits there pensive, his mind wanders back into the past, not so far back, either, when

"Are you listening, Stanley?" Granny raps her knuckles on the table, bringing me back to the present. She can't bear disrespect, even if I'm not doing it on purpose. Or even if I might have been sleeping.

I nod. Nodding is not lying.

Okay. Nodding is lying a little bit, because I really wasn't listening. But nodding is lying with your whole head rather than your mouth, which makes it better.

"That's how you make money, Stan," Stinky Pete says. He reaches for the vinegar pie Mrs. Glashaw dropped off for her husband earlier today.

I can't escape vinegar pie, apparently. First Mrs. Cavanaugh in Manistique would force them on us, and now Mrs. Glashaw.

What have I ever done to deserve such torture? And did Stinky Pete just give me the secret of how to make money and I wasn't listening?

Why, oh, why don't I listen to people? Why have I been tormented with a brain so quick and clever that I can't focus on the little things in life?

"Ahem." Granny passes me a piece of pie that I'm obligated to take since we are in no position to turn down food.

I'm doomed. My life is one misery after another.

"Oh, please," Granny says. Her eyes are rolled up so far in her head they're mostly white. She throws up her hands. "You have to be the most entitled, underappreciative, overdramatic child. . . ." Mama reaches over and pats Granny's hand.

Stinky Pete grins and winks at me before taking a giant bite of pie.

I can't help smiling at that guy.

"So what do you think about what Mr. McLachlan said?" Mama asks, setting her empty plate to the side.

Hmmm. What *do* I think about what Stinky Pete said? I shovel pie into my mouth to give myself a chance to think.

It's not polite to talk with your mouth full.

These people really need to work on their manners.

I chew. Very slowly. It is nothing short of torture. And I still don't know what I think about what Stinky Pete said. Mainly because I didn't hear what Stinky Pete said. I swallow. Very slowly. And clear my throat.

"I think," I say. "I think Stinky Pete has a point." I'm pretty proud of myself for that answer. It's not a lie. In fact, it's the truth, and it sounds like I've been listening all along.

Granny, Mama, and Stinky Pete stare at me as if they want me to keep talking. I take another bite.

I don't know what's worse, Mrs. Glashaw's vinegar pie or trying to figure out what Stinky Pete said while everyone stares at me.

Stinky Pete leans in his chair, his eyes twinkly, his mouth curled at one end. He rests a hand on my arm. "Stan, I said, 'Hard work is the only honest and honorable way to make money.'"

I set down my fork and nod like I agree.

"Archibald Crutchley certainly works hard," Granny says. "And he has a lot of money," she adds, picking up dishes and taking them to the sink.

Stinky Pete's gaze drops to his hands.

Unfortunately, I don't have the time to work hard. I need to make money the fast way or else my name will be Mudd.

I certainly don't mind a little dirt. I just don't want my last name to be Mudd.

I also don't want to give Granny any excuse to wash my face.

Or Crutchley. My name will be Stan Crutchley, a thought so vile my stomach churns.

Or maybe it hurts from the vinegar pie, but either way, I feel sick.

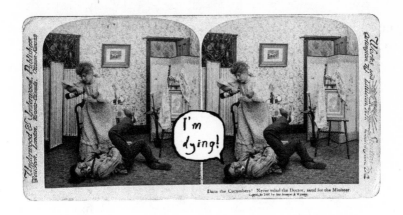

Please don't tell Geri.

Giving the children their suppers.   Copyright 1890 by Geo. Barker.

CHAPTER 12

L ast night, in the middle of the night, I had a brilliant idea. I also had a stomachache.

Vinegar pie. I think vinegar pie could cure Geri. It tastes awful, so it has to be good for you!

I took a piece to Geri early this morning and waved it under her nose, but she didn't flinch. And then I tried to put it in her mouth. Gently. But she would have nothing of it and I made a mess of the sheets and Granny yelled at me later about muddling up Geri's bed.

Also, Geri might still have been asleep.

Then she would have nothing to do with me or the

vinegar pie, so it's another of my brilliant ideas gone to waste.

Luckily I had another brilliant idea during arithmetic class. We were doing the nines times table and one of the questions was "I bought 3 pounds of raisins at 9 cents each. How many cents did they cost?" Which made me think about raisins and then that made me think about rabbit droppings because they look just like raisins.

Rabbit droppings don't taste like raisins, however. Not that I know anything about that.

Then I thought about the time I kicked some rabbit droppings from behind the boardinghouse and all of a sudden I almost jumped out of my coat because a snake quickly slithered through the grass right under my feet.

Which naturally made me think of snake oil. And if I can get some snake oil, my dream of creating a cure for what ails Geri (and making myself rich in the process) is not dead!

Also, those raisins in that math problem ended up costing 27 cents. At least that's what it said when I peeked at Marshall Curtis's paper.

Lucky for me, as Cuddy and I are walking back from getting him a treat and picking up the Carlisles' mail, what should I spy but a real, live snake? It's tiny and cute and slithery. And so harmless.

Well, maybe not completely harmless.

"Cuddy!" I say, pointing. "Look! It's a snake!" I act excited because it's not every day you see a snake sliding along the street.

Cuddy recoils. "It's a snake, Stan! They are dangerous! My uncle was bitten by a snake once and almost didn't live to tell the tale. And he lost a leg and then had to become a pirate."

I have known pirates, and I have no idea why losing a leg would force Cuddy's uncle into becoming one, but that's none of my concern right this moment. I need that snake, or more specifically, I need his oil.

Not this kind of pirate, either.

Just how do you get oil from a snake?

"Um, pick him up, Cuddy," I urge, elbowing him. "My hands are full or I would do it myself," I assure him, spreading the two pieces of mail into both of my hands while moving away from the slimy creature.

Cuddy looks at me like I smell bad and have stolen his last piece of candy.

"You *did* steal my last piece of candy, didn't you, Stan?" he says seriously.

I shake my head and swallow. The candy almost gets stuck in my throat, so I swallow harder and try to smile innocently at the same time. This isn't easy, but somehow it works. I open my mouth to show Cuddy how empty it is of any type of candy. He looks at me skeptically.

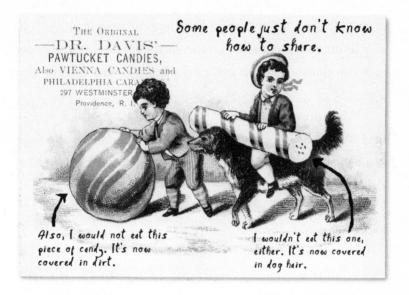

THE ORIGINAL
—DR. DAVIS'—
PAWTUCKET CANDIES,
Also VIENNA CANDIES and
PHILADELPHIA CARA...
297 WESTMINSTER
Providence, R. I.

Some people just don't know how to share.

Also, I would not eat this piece of candy. It's now covered in dirt.

I wouldn't eat this one, either. It's now covered in dog hair.

"I would have given it to you if you had just asked, Stan. Really," he says.

"Well, now I'm asking you to pick up that tiny, cute, harmless snake," I say.

Cuddy finds a stick in the grass and nudges the snake. It's actually not very little. It's about the size of the stick. And it's pretty slimy. And its tongue darts out, hissing. It's all I can do not to squeal and run away like a little girl. I stand on one foot, leaning as far from the deadly viper as I can without looking cowardly.

"Pick it up, Cuddy," I yelp. How in the heck am I going to get oil from this thing?

"I can't, Stan! I can't!" Cuddy drops the stick and jumps like he was just stung by a wasp.

"There are wasps around here?" he cries. Cuddy turns around, flailing his arms and brushing off his hair.

His antics have distracted me. Usually I am attentive, my senses as sharp as knives lying on a bed of nails. But not this time.

"What do we have here?" Mad Madge has snuck up behind us and now holds the snake in her two hands, peering into its face. I take a quick glance around to make sure Nincompoop isn't nearby.

"Nicholas is helping his dad bring in fish down at the docks," she says dismissively.

Now she can read my mind, too?

Mad Madge tears her adoring gaze from the snake to look me square in the face. "Stan, your mind is an open book. Mainly because nothing ever stays secret in that brain of yours. Every thought you have comes straight out your mouth."

Should I argue this with her?

"No, Stan," Cuddy says, shaking his head. He's still waving his arms, shooing off imaginary wasps. "There's no need to argue. She's right."

Madge smiles, switching hands as the snake slithers between them. She leans down to set it free in the grass.

"No!" I yell, stepping closer. Madge stops.

"Why not?" she asks.

It's just a tiny little bee. Nothing to get so worked up over.

"Well, if you must know," I say, using my most educated voice, "the oil of snakes is known to prevent illnesses. And I am planning on oiling this snake."

Mad Madge snorts. "Pfft. How do you oil a snake?" she asks.

Hmmm. That's a good question. I hadn't gotten that far.

"Of course you hadn't. Also, garter snakes aren't the type used for snake oil medicines," she adds, lowering the snake to the ground.

"How do you know, missy?" I huff.

"I investigated a medicine show that was in town a year ago. I wrote a letter to the paper, signed it Mr. John Jones, and that show was run out of town twenty-four hours later. It was one of my proudest moments. Too bad no one would have taken me seriously if I had signed my own name."

Madge brushes her hands on her dress before tucking a wisp of hair behind her ear. When she's not threatening me with bodily harm, she actually looks kind of pleasant. And now that I'm close to her, I can admit she doesn't smell too bad. In fact, she smells good. A little like the lilac bush behind the mercantile.

Wait! What am I thinking here? We're talking about Mad Madge! Violent criminal! Head gangster! Thief! Bully!

"You think I smell good?" she asks. I can't tell if she's accusing me or flattered.

"He does," Cuddy says, his hands still flailing. His arms have got to be getting tired. "And he always says your hair looks like the shiny coal we pick up along the train tracks. You know, how it sparkles and . . . Hey!" Cuddy says as I push him to the ground.

"Oops!"

It was an accident. Kind of.

I made sure he fell on a soft spot where the pale grass is already sprouting up and the dirt below is no longer frozen.

At least I hope it was a soft spot. He hasn't moved since he accidentally fell.

Mad Madge eyes me thoughtfully. I clear my throat. Cuddy lies on his back, spread eagle, moaning.

"I'm injured, Stan! Help me! I'm dying!"

"There are snakes in that grass," I remind him. He immediately hops up, brushing dirt from his trousers.

"So why do you need snake oil?" Mad Madge's eyes

squint. I know that look. It's the one that always comes before a bunch of nosy questions.

"Um, n-no reason," I stammer. "Uh, see you tomorrow?" I grab Cuddy's arm and drag him toward his house.

"Bye, Mad Madge!" he yells. I jerk him a little. "She doesn't look that mad, Stan," he says, stumbling to keep up.

"We don't say that to her face," I hiss. I sneak a glance at Mad Madge. She catches my eye, her mouth hooked in a slight smile.

Which, for some reason, makes me feel more scared than when she was threatening to beat me up.

Pretty sure the cat is winning.

This child is not even focusing.
Put down the ball!

CHAPTER 13

"Can you come in today, Stan? Is today the day? Can I show you what Uncle Cuthbert got me? You will be surprised!" Cuddy wiggles his eyebrows as he jumps from foot to foot.

"Sure, Cuddy," I laugh. That guy can be such a card. Also, Cuddy can't keep a secret to save his life, so a surprise is certainly unusual. We climb the steps to his house. The door swings open before I can even reach for the handle, and there is Mrs. Law, staring at us over the rims of her spectacles.

"You're late," she pronounces. She reaches between Cuddy and me and ushers Cuddy in, then points a finger in my face. "I'm not sure why you're still needed, but if it were up to me, Cuddy would no longer be in your care."

I hear Cuddy protest, but arguing with Mrs. Law is like playing chess with a cat; no matter how good you are at chess, sooner or later the cat will just knock over all the pieces and act like he's won. Before I know it, I'm staring at a large wooden door.

I have a feeling Mrs. Law has never lost an argument. Or a chess game.

I take each stair slowly and sit for a minute on the bottom step. I have failed at all my moneymaking schemes and might end up losing the only real paying job I've ever had. I am not, apparently, cut out to be a gangster or a snake oil salesman. I don't have time to make money through hard work, which is a ridiculous idea anyway, no offense, Stinky Pete.

I pick up a handful of pebbles and fling them into the street, one by one, trying to hit the lamppost across from the house. Ping. Ping.

"Yes, well, Margaret." I hear Mr. Carlisle's voice booming from the open window behind me and pause midthrow. "I appreciate the fact that you want me home, but Captain Slater has the *Wanderer* moored at the docks and I can't leave him alone down there." Mumbles follow as Cuddy's mom responds, but I'm no longer paying attention.

Did Mr. Carlisle say Captain *Slater*? As in *Arthur Slater*? Hero of the seas? As in my father? I drop the rest of the pebbles, pop up from the step, and hightail it to the docks.

I knew it! I knew my father was someone special, great, and heroic! Because where else would I have come from?

"Maybe your mother?" I jump. Mad Madge is leaning against the bank building, cleaning her fingernails with a jackknife. She's as sneaky as, well, as I was when I stole my lucky hat back from Geri.

To be perfectly honest, it *is* my lucky hat. And since I retrieved it, my luck has changed already! I found my dad! Also, Geri doesn't even need the hat anymore. She's feeling so much better that yesterday alone she diagnosed me with five different illnesses and one I'm sure she made up.

"Oh! So that's where the hat went! I wondered." Geri appears from behind Madge, her hands in her pockets, her hair trying to escape her braids. How do these two know each other? The only thing that could make this scene any worse is if Nincompoop and Granny showed up. I peer around cautiously, planning my getaway.

"Oh, Nicholas isn't here. He had to mind his brothers," Madge says, folding up her knife and sticking it in her coat. "And Geri and I met the other day at school. Remember? You introduced us."

I think I would have remembered that.

"But what's this about your father?" she asks in her

journalist voice. I'm pretty sure she's one step away from grabbing her notebook and pencil.

I don't dare look at Geri. She's been hearing misinformation about my dad since before I even knew he was still alive, and I can practically hear her eyes cranking up into her head.

"Well, I overheard Cuddy's dad saying a Captain Slater is down at the docks." I feel like springing out of my shoes with excitement.

Madge scratches something into her notebook. "Go on," she says without looking up.

"Stan," Geri says in her warn-y voice. Her warn-y voice is very annoying, I don't mind saying. Actually, her entire voice is very annoying.

I don't mind saying that, either.

Madge and Geri glare at me.

Did I say that aloud?

"Yes, yes, you did, Stan. Apologize." Madge steps toward me.

Geri lays a hand on Madge's arm, stopping her midstride. "We are not going down this road again, Stan. Do you hear me?"

I glance up and down the street. Of course we're going down this road again. It's State Street! You can't get anywhere if you don't go down this road.

Girls. Sheesh. It's true, as Mr. Crutchley is fond of saying, that lady folk just aren't very good with directions.

"Stan." Geri's shoulders hunch, her palms open and

flailing. "What will it take for you to realize your mother is the best thing you've got going? And Peter McLachlan would walk over burning hot coals for you. And Granny"—I cock my eyebrows at her at the mention of Granny—"okay, we'll leave Granny out of it. But, my point is, your father is not worth knowing, Stan." Her voice cracks, and I nod as if I agree. But Mama, Stinky Pete, and Granny aren't my father, my real, honest-to-goodness father. For one thing, two of them are girls, and the other has "stinky" in his name.

THINGS GIRLS CAN DO:

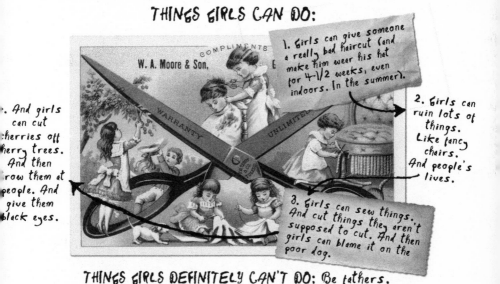

1. Girls can give someone a really bad haircut (and make him wear his hat for 4-1/2 weeks, even indoors. In the summer).

2. Girls can ruin lots of things. Like fancy chairs. And people's lives.

. And girls can cut cherries off cherry trees. And then throw them at people. And give them black eyes.

3. Girls can sew things. And cut things they aren't supposed to cut. And then girls can blame it on the poor dog.

THINGS GIRLS DEFINITELY CAN'T DO: Be fathers.

"Are you listening to me, Stan? I will tell Granny if you even think about going down to that dock and seeing someone who may or may not turn out to be your father. And then you probably won't be allowed to set foot outside the house except to go to school and bring Cuddy home." She shakes a finger at me. I nod like I see her point.

I don't see her point.

I let her and Mad Madge steer me toward the boarding-house. They chatter on about becoming a doctor like Elizabeth Blackwell and a journalist like Nellie Bly. Blah, blah, blah. I don't even take the time to remind them these are not occupations for ladies.

look! All boys!

FACULTY OF THE COLLEGE OF PHYSICIANS AND SURGEONS,
OF THE UNIVERSITY OF THE STATE OF NEW YORK.
New York.

look! All the doctors are boys, too!

Instead, I take a peek at the docks as we walk by. Tall masts jut over the fishing boats and poke over the top of the steamships, bouncing on the waves like fingers beckoning, and I just know my dad is there, waiting for me.

My day was as dumb as this guy's hair. And just about as messy.

I couldn't help it. I got up late.

CHAPTER 14

Today was the dumbest day of my life.

"You mean, today you were the dumbest you've ever been in your life?" Geri asks. Cuddy snickers, and I give him the evil eye. Which only makes him giggle even more. He starts choking on his cinnamon stick.

I, apparently, am not a whiz at the evil eye. I smack Cuddy on the back. He coughs before licking his candy again.

"No, that's not at all what I mean," I clarify. Cuddy slinks his hand into mine. "What I mean is that the day was so looong."

"Well, at least you didn't have to endure forty-five minutes of Mr. Servis's lecture on human nature and science, which was so out of date I swear he said the earth is flat and the sun revolves around us," Geri says, her words a rapid-fire exhale.

Now that she's feeling better, she insists on attending school even though there are only a few weeks left. Who does that?

"And the school doesn't even have any lab equipment! How will I do experiments?" She throws her arms up in frustration. Her hair looks like an experiment; stray curls stick out from under her hat every which way. "And then he started talking about miasma and how we should avoid bad air because it will make us sick, so I, of course, mentioned that germ theory is in general acceptance by anyone knowledgeable in the scientific community, and he just patted my head and dismissed us for lunch."

Cuddy licks his fingers and sticks his hand back in mine. I try not to think about germs.

We near the docks, busy with freight and fish and trains. I stop in my tracks. A two-masted schooner bobs next to the merchandise dock like an apple in a barrel of water.

"Oh. I don't like that bobbing-for-apples game, Stan," Cuddy says. "I almost drowned once playing it." I pull on his hand to go closer to the ship. It's one I haven't seen before, and *Wanderer* is plainly painted on its stern.

I'm drawn toward it like a fish in a net being hauled in, helpless.

But apparently I'm more like a fish on a hook snagged

on a rock, because I'm not moving. Cuddy is surprisingly strong for someone so little.

"I can't go on the docks, Stan," Cuddy reminds me. "Remember? I'm not allowed." He tugs on my arm.

"You are not going there, Stan," Geri says, her voice a dead-on impression of Granny. She glares at me. Cuddy pulls me toward town, yanking me with his sticky, germ-infested hands.

"Let's go. Cuddy needs to get home. Now," Geri says firmly.

I look at the ship. Men amble up and down the dock, some of them stopping to slap each other on the backs, others hauling crates on and off boats.

These are my people. I should be there, slapping people and hauling things.

"Oh, I'm happy to slap you, if that's what you're missing in your life," Geri says.

I flinch. She's so violent for someone who wants to be a doctor.

"Stan!" All three of us swing our necks around to see who is calling me. Could it be my dad? Did he recognize me?

"Over here!" I peer down the railroad tracks and spy Stinky Pete, his shiny teeth sparkling in the spring sun.

Geri relaxes when she sees him, and Cuddy jumps up and down, waving with both arms.

"Hey, I've gotta go see Stinky Pete," I say, jogging off in his direction. "Um." I turn to Geri and point at Cuddy. "See that he gets home, okay?"

"Stan! Don't you dare!" Geri warns.

I wave, ignoring Geri's openmouthed expression and Cuddy's slumped shoulders, and head toward my friend.

"Just going to spend some time with Stinky Pete!" I yell behind me.

When I get closer to Stinky Pete and can no longer hear Geri's protests, I slow down and take a quick peek at Cuddy and Geri returning to town. She is holding Cuddy's hand. I'll bet he is over the moon.

At least that's what I tell myself, because right about now I don't feel so good. I feel a little like the time I told Nincompoop his mother must have a really loud bark.

He stood there with his arm cocked and his fist ready to slug me in the gut, but the minute I said that, he froze, dropped his arm, squeezed his eyes shut, and grimaced like *I* had slugged *him.* Then he ran off down the street.

"What did you just do?" Mad Madge said accusingly.

"Listen! He was about to punch me in the stomach!" I protested.

"Nicholas's mother just left them!" Madge said. "He can't sleep at night. He can't focus at school." She took her ever-present pencil and thrust it in my face. "Nicholas wouldn't hurt a fly, but if I weren't a lady I'd slug you myself."

I feel now like I felt then. Like a punch in the gut might have been a better option.

Stinky Pete saunters up and sets a crate down on one

Aaah! I hope he'd hurt this fly! It's horrifying!

of the rails. "What's up, my man?" he asks with a smile.

"Oh, um, just taking Cuddy home from school and, well, you know, keeping Geri out of trouble." My eyes dart toward the *Wanderer.* Some sailors are by the ramp leading up to the ship. Is one my dad?

I'm well aware I can't let Stinky Pete see my gaze. He's overly cautious about keeping me safe, especially since that unfortunate dynamite accident at the lumber camp.

Although we both know it was certainly not my fault the uncoordinated Archibald Crutchley fell in the river and almost died.

"Except for the fact that you kind of pushed him in," Stinky Pete reminds me.

I wave him off with a shake of my head. "Well, he shouldn't have been standing so close to the shore," I say.

Stinky Pete nods good-naturedly. "Let bygones be bygones, hey, son?" he says, jacking the crate onto his shoulder.

"Where are you going?" I ask. I wonder if he is going on the dock. And if he is, perhaps I can tag along. And if I tag along, maybe I can get close to the *Wanderer* and my father. And then . . . I don't know what will happen then.

But I'll cross that bridge when I come to it.

I'm a whiz at crossing bridges, I don't mind saying.

"I'm delivering some freight," Stinky Pete says. "Wanna come along?"

I nod so hard my eyeballs feel jittery.

"Well, c'mon then, but stay right with me. There are a lot of ways to get in trouble on the docks," Stinky Pete says seriously. I'm just about sure I would never get in trouble.

"How about last week when you got in trouble with your teacher for writing fake love letters to people who didn't even like each other?" Stinky Pete asks.

I put my hand over my mouth to muffle a laugh. That was so funny. I put a love note on Miss Wenzel's desk from Mr. Servis, and when she opened it her face turned the color of Mad Madge's red woolen scarf.

I hadn't realized, however, that Mr. Servis is a married man. Or that Miss Wenzel would recognize my handwriting. Or that Mama would tell Stinky Pete.

But I have seen the light and come to Jesus. And I asked forgiveness and I wrote "Stanley Slater will not forge notes or anything else ever again or risk expulsion" one hundred times on the blackboard. Which is a poorly constructed sentence, if you ask me. But, of course, no one ever asks me.

"Yeah, well, that was, um, an accident?" I say.

Stinky Pete shakes his head, but his mouth turns up and he walks along like a fellow with a song in his head. He nods for me to follow him.

I'm on the docks. I'm on the docks. I'm on the docks.

I'm actually facedown on the docks because I tripped on a railroad tie, but I'm still on the docks.

I sure hope my dad didn't see that. I don't want him to think his son is clumsy.

Stinky Pete chuckles and lends me a hand, hauling me up with one arm. "You hurt?" he asks.

"Nah," I answer, brushing coal dust off my trousers.

It's possible someone tripped me

Aaah!

Because I am usually very light on my feet.

Stinky Pete takes off, whistling and talking about the latest news and how when he returned to the real world after the river drive, he was sad to hear about Frederick Douglass's death.

"He was an amazing man, Stan," Stinky Pete says. "Brave and intelligent. A big supporter of women's suffrage."

"He wanted women to suffer?" I ask. I can think of a few women who could stand to suffer a little bit, but for the most part, I don't think suffering is a good thing.

Stinky Pete laughs. "No, no. It means he supported a woman's right to vote," he explains.

Did not want women to suffer. Apparently never met Geri. Or Granny.

Mr. Frederick Douglass

"I heard Mr. Crutchley talking to Granny and both of them think women aren't smart enough to vote."

Stinky Pete suddenly stops. A big sigh escapes his lips like smoke from Mr. Glashaw's cigar. "Let's take a moment and think of the women and girls in your life. You've got your mother, Geri, that Madge girl . . ." Stinky Pete ticks off names. "You think they aren't smart enough to vote?" He picks up his pace again.

To tell God's honest truth, they could probably run the entire country and arrange the stars in the heavens to spell out Bible verses, if they put their minds to it. But I'm afraid cat's got my tongue right at the moment. Now I'm the one suddenly stopped in his tracks. On the railroad tracks. And not because I don't want to admit girls are smart, either.

I really don't want to admit girls are smart.

No. The real reason is I'm next to the *Wanderer*. And next to the *Wanderer* is my father. Another wanderer.

Who is now found. And doesn't need to wander any longer.

CHAPTER 15

How do I know that's my father? Because everyone gathers around him in wonder like it's dark and he's a firefly stuck in a jar.

Oops. I need to let those fireflies out as soon as I get home.

Also, he's the biggest man on the docks—strong, brave, and manly.

Just like me.

And he's wearing a captain's hat. And I overheard someone call him Cap'n Slater.

I pull myself together and slink behind the closest stack of crates. I briefly think about Stinky Pete, wondering if he's still talking about all that unnecessary information like voting and women and people who have died, but he's a big boy. He can take care of himself; I can't always be taking care of everyone.

"Woo-hoo! So, Cap'n, we off until morning?" I hear spit hitting planks and the smack of hand against skin.

"Wha—? What was that for?" a voice asks. I peer carefully around the crates to see the good captain with his hands on the sailor's collar, glaring nose to nose into his eyes. The sailor looks like a boy, almost like Nincompoop, smaller still, standing next to the captain. My dad. The boy holds a hand to his cheek.

"You mind all of your manners, Joey, even if you have very few. At least while we're in town. And keep a low profile. No spitting. No hollering. You hear?" the captain hisses. "We can't afford attention."

Joey lowers his hands carefully, shoving them in his pockets and hunching his neck into his shoulders. He reminds me of one of the kittens at home, the runt who can't get any milk. The one Geri brought inside and has been hand-feeding.

I might bring the guy some milk. But he'll have to feed himself.

"Sorry, Cap'n," he says, staring through the cracks below his feet.

"Sorry, nothin'," my dad answers. I'm not positive this is my dad, now that I think about it. I don't think my dad would be so mean. I rise from my crouch only to sink back down when I see a lady strolling the dock, arm in arm with a nicely dressed gentleman.

It's Mr. and Mrs. Angell, the photographer and his wife; she is the biggest flibbertigibbet in all the town. Last week, when Geri and I were walking to school, I may or may not have called Geri a spleeny, fly-bitten hedgepig. In my defense, she said there was no more bacon and then proceeded to pull three pieces from her pocket and wouldn't share.

Anyway, Mrs. Angell happened to hear me, and by the time I got to school Miss Wenzel knew the entire story, made me write "I will not call people spleeny, fly-bitten hedgepigs" one hundred times on the blackboard, and then made me stand with my nose in the *o* of the word "not" for a half hour.

That's a long time to stand with your nose in an *o*. Especially when Mad Madge kept asking me questions: Who did I call a name? Why did I choose that name? How did Miss Wenzel find out? On and on, jotting notes the whole time.

Also, I wasn't calling *people* a name; I was calling Geri a name. And I was hungry.

The captain, my dad, is still shouting at Joey, who looks smaller and smaller every time I sneak a peek at him. "You take even one minuscule step out of line, boy, and I swear on my good mother's name you will be food for the fishes." I hear another smack, a sharp breath, and my father again. "I swear, calling you stupid would be an insult to stupid people." Then he actually does swear.

I should probably curse more. It's apparently a family trait.

Mr. and Mrs. Angell come closer and I hide, peeking my head just a teensy bit out the side. My dad still holds Joey's collar. Joey's head hangs loosely, his hat twisting in his hands, when all of a sudden my dad loosens his hold, straightens up, and beams a grin so bright I swear the temperature rises fifteen degrees. He clamps an arm around Joey like they are the best of buddies.

I'm not sure I like this sudden friendship.

Plus, what just happened?

"Ma'am?" my dad says. His voice is as sweet as the candy that makes Cuddy so sticky. He tips his cap with a smile. All of a sudden he seems to be a completely different fellow from the one threatening Joey just a minute before.

Joey smiles, too. Until the Angells walk by with a nod. Then my dad knocks Joey on the side of his head and turns toward town.

"Don't you dare leave this post," he tosses over his shoulder. "I'll be back later."

Joey rubs his neck and sits on a crate by the gangplank with a sigh. I know the feeling. I stand up with a sigh, my dad a fair distance ahead of me.

I have to follow him.

Far off at the other end of the dock, I spy Stinky Pete talking to Mr. and Mrs. Angell, gesturing frantically and looking all around like he's lost something valuable. I leave him alone for five minutes and he's already lost something. I briefly wonder what he's lost, but I pretend not to see him as I sneak around barrels and crates and keep my dad in my sight. I don't have time to worry about Stinky Pete right now. I have a father to follow.

I spot him, straight ahead, tipping his cap to all the ladies he approaches. They smile in return. One lady even curtsies and giggles behind a gloved hand.

Why is he paying all this attention to the ladies? What about the dog tripping along behind him?

Just as I think this, my dad stoops down, pulls something from his pocket, gives it to the dog, and pats him gently.

He is a hero. He is a hero who cares about stray dogs. He probably has a heart of gold and that business with Joey was an accident.

My dad keeps patting the dog while glancing at all the people on the street. When Miss Beasley approaches, he takes a second look before standing up again.

He should be careful. Everyone says Miss Beasley could

talk the ear off a donkey. Which I wouldn't mind seeing if I didn't feel so bad about the donkey.

As we get closer to town, however, I start to notice something else. None of the men seem to want to talk to my dad. In fact, they move away from him as if he's Moses and they are the Red Sea.

I'm not sure I understand. I love my mama, but I certainly didn't get my charming personality from her. And if that's the case, I must have inherited it from my father.

But the men seem to be trying to avoid charming Captain Slater, hero of the seas. Even the bicycle club, barreling down State Street—all nine of them seem to spy my dad at the same time and veer so sharply around him, one runs into the boardwalk in front of the Central Hotel.

To be fair, they aren't the most athletic group of men.

Instead of lending the poor guy a hand, my father skips up the steps and opens the door to the billiard room, releasing a cloud of smoke. A man leaving the hotel spies my dad and draws back like he's spied Genghis Khan himself and he's wearing a captain's hat.

Let's make this clear. My father is not Genghis Khan. He's the captain of a ship, a manly man, a hero. And perhaps in his off time, he's a sheriff and these men are all wanted by the law.

You and your luggage are wanted by the law, missy!

Or he's a detective and these men are all wanted by the law.

Or he's a well-respected preacher and these men all need their very souls saved. Because they're all wanted by the law.

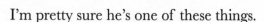

I'm pretty sure he's one of these things.

I run and help the fellow onto his bicycle, and he rides away with a brief thanks and no retreating glance. I gingerly step toward the window, the one with TOLEDO AND MILWAUKEE BEER SOLD HERE on the front, and peer in.

Not obviously, of course. I am sneaky. I'm sly as a fox. As sneaky as one of Pinkerton's detectives.

I'm a whiz at being sneaky, I don't mind saying. And unseen. I should be a detective.

Except someone has seen me. And his large, solid hand plops onto my shoulder like a poached egg on toast. Except not as runny. I look up to see Stinky Pete.

Also, I'm hungry.

"You can't take off on me like that, Stan. Especially on the docks. You near 'bout gave me a heart attack." He looks stern. Or about as stern as a guy with twinkly eyes can look. "C'mon. Time to get home before your mother kills us both."

I reluctantly turn from the window but not before I catch a last glimpse of my father. He's alone at the bar talking to the bartender. His finger points at him like a pistol and the bartender is unmoving, midswipe of the counter, like a man before a firing squad. He looks like he might cry.

What kind of fellow cries?

"I do," Stinky Pete says, steering me toward the boarding-house. "There's no shame in crying."

I like this guy, I really do, but I'm pretty sure my father doesn't cry. Although it seems like people around him might.

I'm not sure which is better.

If you're not too busy,
St. Mary, I could really
use your help.

CHAPTER 16

Where did you go? And why did you forsake your responsibilities for Cuddy and just assume I would pick up the slack? I demand an explanation." Geri is one inch from my nose, and her eyes bore into mine.

She might be the one related to my father, because she is scary. Scary Geri.

Geri's chin drops. "What did you call me?" Her lips barely move.

"Um. I said, 'Hail Mary.' Yep, that's what I said." I nod forcefully and look at her without blinking.

"Hail Mary? Like the prayer?"

"Exactly!" I'm glad we understand one another.

"We're not even Catholic!" she splutters. I nod again. That's true, but that doesn't mean we can't pray. "I swear, if I wasn't worried about how much stress your mother is under, I would go to her immediately and tell her the shenanigans you've been up to."

I keep my mouth shut. Sometimes, I've found, that's the only way to win with Geri.

And by win, I mean not have her tell your mama things you'd rather she didn't know.

Geri leans in so close our foreheads practically touch, and I breathe in her hot breath. "Don't you dare neglect Cuddy again, Stan." I nod. "Because it is very, very important to be a responsible member of society, not someone who leeches off everyone else. No one likes leeches." She turns on her heel and marches off to her room. Probably to read some boring medical book and find a disease she can kill me with.

"She's right, you know," Stinky Pete says. I hadn't seen him sitting there in the dark living room. He's been staying at the boardinghouse since he took a job at the Martel Furnace Company. I will admit, I like having him here, and not just because of the bossy women who show up every time I blink, but also because if he wasn't here, I wouldn't have anyone to beat in cribbage. Mr. Glashaw usually forgets we're playing halfway through our game, gets up to use the washroom, and then doesn't return. Which is bad sportsmanship, if you ask me.

But I'm not too happy with Stinky Pete when he agrees with Geri. We're supposed to be on the same side here.

"But she's right," he repeats. "You have a responsibility to the Carlisle family, and caring for someone's child is nothing to take lightly. You should always do what's right. You might not get recognition for it, but you will be able to sleep at night."

I don't know what he's talking about. I'm a whiz at sleeping, I don't mind saying. In fact, I could take a nap right now.

Stinky Pete pats the sofa. "C'mon. Have a seat."

I plop down next to him, not even stopping myself from leaning my head against his shoulder, his solid, plaid shoulder.

Stinky Pete wraps his arm around me and opens his book, settling into the sofa like he's one of the cushions.

I don't feel good about today, that's a fact. I don't feel right about abandoning Cuddy to Geri and her wily ways. But I couldn't help it. I had to find out more about my father, because what if this is my last chance? What if he sails away and I never see him again?

Stinky Pete shifts and flips the page. I glance down at his lap. His bookmark is a tattered

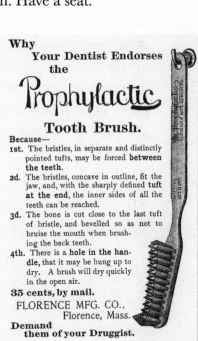

Why **Your Dentist Endorses** the

Prophylactic

Tooth Brush.

Because—

1st. The bristles, in separate and distinctly pointed tufts, may be forced **between the teeth.**

2d. The bristles, concave in outline, fit the jaw, and, with the sharply defined **tuft at the end,** the inner sides of all the teeth can be reached.

3d. The bone is cut close to the last tuft of bristle, and bevelled so as not to bruise the mouth when brushing the back teeth.

4th. There is a **hole in the handle,** that it may be hung up to dry. A brush will dry quickly in the open air.

35 cents, by mail.

FLORENCE MFG. CO., Florence, Mass.

Demand them of your **Druggist.**

Stinky Pete's teeth are so shiny, he must brush them 45 times a day.

piece of paper, worn with use. I don't care what it says, of course, but my eyes are pulled to the writing, scratched in black ink and faded:

> *To know what is right and not do it is the worst cowardice.*
> — *Confucius*

I squeeze my eyes shut. It's too much. Do I even know what's right? And is this Confucius guy saying I'm a coward?

He has the perfect name, because Confucius is confusing.

My brain spins like an out-of-control top. I think about taking care of Mama. About my dad. About money. About how maybe my dad might be the answer to our problems with money. About someone named Confucius and how you get to be one of those people known by one name. I might want to be one of those people. Stanucius. Maybe someday Stinky Pete will use one of my quotes as a bookmark.

> Don't trust anyone whose name rhymes with "scary."
> — Stanucius

> I'm a whiz at lots of things, I don't mind saying.
> — Stanucius

> Bacon. — Stanucius

Dads should not be allowed to leave their kids.
— Stanucius

I'm not the only one who doesn't like to tie his shoes.

CHAPTER 17

I must have fallen asleep on the sofa. One of Granny's crocheted afghans covers me and I smell bacon wafting in from the kitchen.

What time is it?

"It's five minutes until we leave for school, you ninny hammer." Geri sits on the stool near the door, tying her shoes. I rub my eyes, my poor, tired eyes.

Wait! Who on earth is she to call me a ninny hammer?

"Well, you're a . . . you're a . . ."

Geri stops tying her shoe and stares at me. "Go on. What am I?" she challenges.

"You're a girl!" It's all I can come up with on such short notice. Plus, I'm a slow waker-upper.

Geri raises an eyebrow just as Mama comes out of the kitchen with three slices of bacon between a couple pieces of toast. "Here you go, honey. Take this with you. You're going to be late picking up Cuddy." She hands me my coat and hustles me through the door so quickly I barely have time to tie my shoes.

"Your shoes are untied, Stan," Geri says primly. Like she's so perfect. Also, have you ever tried to tie your shoes while holding two pieces of dry toast and some bacon in your mouth?

"No, can't say as I have," Geri responds. "Nor will I probably ever have the opportunity, seeing as I'm always prepared and never running late."

We trudge on toward the Third Ward School. I chomp on my bacon and choke down my toast and always, always keep my eyes peeled for Mad Madge, of course. I'm always very alert.

It's my natural spy ability.

Also, I don't feel like answering her endless questions this morning.

"Boo!" I nearly jump out of my skin. Mad Madge comes up behind me—sneaky Mad Madge.

"IT LOOKS LIKE A PLOT ON OUR TELEGRAPH LINES!"

"You should not sneak up on people," I huff. "It's not polite!"

"I hardly snuck up on you," she replies. "I've been calling your name for the last block."

Hmmm. Maybe I should work on my hearing.

"I was just waiting to see how long it would take you to notice," Geri says. She hands Madge a slice of bacon from her pocket and sticks her nose back in her book. "Morning," she says. They share a smile.

"So do you have last night's homework done?" Madge asks.

Is she talking to me?

"Yes, I'm talking to you."

Homework? As in work to take home? What kind of evil plot is this?

"Yes, *homework.*" She emphasizes each syllable. Slowly. As if I don't know what she's talking about.

I have no idea what she's talking about.

"Well, I hope you do have it done; otherwise you'll miss recess and have to stay after school," Madge warns.

I hope I have it done, too! I can't stay after school. I have to get Cuddy and then go spy on my dad. I have business to attend to.

"Hey, where is your no-good excuse for a cousin?" I suddenly notice Nincompoop is missing.

Madge shrugs. "He's done with school for the year. And I don't know if he'll come back in the fall. His dad needs help on the fishing boat."

Now, this is some interesting news! What if my dad needs

help on his boat? Would I be able to quit school and spend my days on the high seas instead? Would I be the next Captain Slater, hero of the Great Lakes?

"Ha!" Geri scoffs. "You'd be lucky if the crew didn't throw you off as bait."

I glare at her.

"Wait. Your dad isn't the same Slater who's the captain of the *Wanderer*, is he?" Madge asks, stopping midstride. Probably because he is that famous. And amazing.

I nod. Perhaps a little proudly.

Madge's jaw drops. "Wow."

I nod. Even a little more proudly. "I know," I say knowingly, even though I'm not exactly sure what I know.

"He's famous," she whispers.

"He is?" I gasp.

"Yes," she continues. "Or should I say *in*famous?"

She can say whatever she wants because this is great news! Plus, what's the difference between famous and infamous? They're both obviously amazing.

"There's a big difference between the two words, Stan," Geri says, shooing us along. "Being famous is a good thing. Being infamous means almost the same thing, except rather than being known for doing good, you're famous for all the bad stuff you do."

"What is my dad known for?" I ask. I rub the spot between my eyebrows. Do I even want to know?

Madge glances at Geri, then looks at me. "He's a criminal, Stan. A mean-as-a-snake, ruthless criminal."

A criminal? "What? What has he done?" I ask.

"He's done a lot of things, Stan. But the reason he's in town now, restocking his ship, is that he's a timber pirate."

"Pfft," I snort. This can't be right. She's making it all up. These are the Great Lakes, not Robert Louis Stevenson's *Treasure Island,* where pirates sail the seas with their peg legs and parrots. My dad

Maybe he's more like this kind of famous?

NO!

didn't have a limp or an earring or any birds perched on his shoulder.

"No, he's more like *Dr. Jekyll and Mr. Hyde*," Geri mumbles.

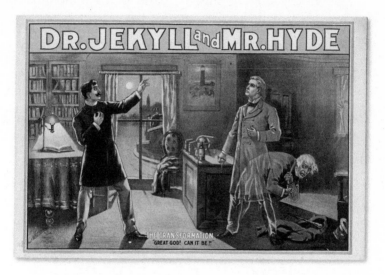

(This doesn't look promising.)

"Awful Arthur was not given that name for nothing," Madge adds. She clutches her books and picks up the pace. I huff to keep up.

"Who calls him Awful Arthur?" I ask. That's not a very complimentary name, even I must admit.

"All the guys down at the docks. Just not to his face."

Okay. Now I understand. Madge is definitely making this up to scare me. To make me think my dad is something other than a manly, trustworthy hero. Geri probably put her up to it.

"Oh, he's successful. No one can catch him red-handed, and word on the docks is that he's got ties to gangsters in Chicago," Madge adds. Geri nods in agreement.

"How do you know this?" I stand in the middle of the street, exasperated. They are girls. They can't have spent time on the docks; no self-respecting girl would be seen down there.

"First of all, as a future journalist, it's my job to find things out. And second, all my brothers plus my dad work on the docks, and they gossip more than your grandmother's quilting group down at the church."

What? Granny is part of a quilting group? Why don't I know any of these things?

"Where do you think the new quilt on your bed came from?" Geri sighs. She holds her book like she's about to hit me on the head with it.

I never really thought about it. Sure, that quilt showed

up on my bed last week unannounced and very appreciated. But I don't like to ask too many unnecessary questions— usually they lead to other unnecessary questions. And those usually lead to me getting in trouble.

Madge shakes her head. "There's no such thing as an unnecessary question, Stan. Also, Geri, I owe you an apology; he *is* as thick as a tree trunk."

"I accept," Geri responds.

I try to pretend they don't exist. Which isn't easy since they're standing right next to me and don't ever stop talking. But Madge knows things about my father and I am curious.

"So what can you tell me about this timber pirate you obviously made up?" I ask. At this point I don't even care— I'll take any information about my father, even lies.

Madge exhales like Geri does when talking to me for more than three and a half minutes. "Facts are facts, Stan. Your dad is bad news. Timber pirates steal wood from wharves and storehouses and boats and then unload it in places like Chicago. I think you should stay away from him. Although," she says, a bit of sneak edging her voice, "if you want to arrange an interview for me, I would be forever grateful."

"No!" Geri says forcefully. "Both of you. Stay away from that man."

Madge shakes her head as if coming out of a bad dream. "Oh, of course! You're right, Geri. I don't know what I was thinking." She turns to me. "Listen to Geri, Stan. Stay away."

Like I would take advice from my personal bully. Or my cousin, who is always trying to infect me with deadly diseases.

"Stan!" Why are people always calling my name? And why do they always do it when I'm busy with other things? Important things, like making a decision about what my name should be when I turn to a life of crime: Stan the Atrocious? Stan the Horrible? Stan the Hun, whatever a hun is? Fearless Stan? I need something that will strike terror in the hearts of namby-pamby, so-called men.

"How about Fear*ful* Stan?" Madge mutters. I choose to ignore her, however. It's not polite to punch a girl, plus, I'm pretty sure she can beat me up.

"Stan!" I look up the street and see Cuddy running our way, his stubby legs churning down the muddy road.

"I was afraid you were going to be late, so I told Mother and Grandmother I heard you coming," Cuddy wheezes. I notice mud on his trousers. I'll probably be blamed for that when I drop him off. "And can you come in after school to see my surprise?" He trots after Geri like a faithful puppy. A very talkative, faithful puppy.

"Hi, Geri," he sighs. She smiles and pats his head.

I nod, but my mind is on other things. My dad is a criminal. A gangster. Also, last night after dinner, Mama went for a ride with Mr. Crutchley in his new carriage. Stinky Pete clomped up to his room without saying a word for the rest of the evening, and I was left with Geri and Granny and a drip of water that kept plopping on my head as I washed dishes. Granny said it's because we need a new roof.

I know we don't have the money for a new roof. I know Mr. Crutchley definitely *does* have the money for a new roof. I know I don't want Mr. Crutchley's money and everything else that comes with it, so I have come up with some brilliant moneymaking ideas. The problem is, they might not be completely legal.

Granny's hair in the morning

Stop staring. It's not that bad.

CHAPTER 18

I've decided that school is for lily-livered milksops. And we all know I am not one of *them*.

Plus, my homework wasn't done and I might soon be leaving for a life on the high seas. Or lakes. Or any body of water that will take me.

I told the girls I needed to see Cuddy to the door of his classroom, and then snuck out the back of the school. Now, for some reason, I find myself lingering on the street in front of the merchandise dock, watching my dad's ship rise with the swells. I take a deep breath and step onto the dock. It seems like it's rocking with the waves, or maybe it's just my nerves.

I have nerves of steel. I probably inherited them from my dad.

Except all of a sudden I feel like I have to go to the privy. Here comes my dad. Straight for me, his gaze as sharp as Madge's pencil and just about as pointy. His finger is aimed directly at me, and his mouth is set in an unbending line.

I have nowhere to hide. I am frozen to this spot. My dad's finger is scarier than Granny's head before she straightens her hair in the morning.

"Son!" Did he really call me that? Did he recognize me from my ruggedly handsome good looks? Or my witty sense of humor? Or my steely, manly nerves? I wave, but I still can't move.

"You, boy!" he says as he gets closer. "I need you to do me a favor." He smiles and his whole face changes, like when Mama pulls back the curtains and the bedroom loses its shadow and feels as welcoming as a warm slice of fresh bread.

My stomach growls. I would like a warm slice of fresh bread.

"Well, I might be able to do something about that." My dad grins, clamping me on the shoulder. His arm feels heavy, like the oxen yoke I once tried on at the Heberts' farm back in Manistique.

I couldn't get it off and Geri wouldn't help me, even though she supposedly wants to be a doctor. Then Old Farmer Hebert showed up and yelled at me, but he also loosened the bow so I could get my head out.

Then I ran home. And Geri called me Stuckley in front of all my friends and I couldn't leave the house for one month and four days without someone reminding me of that unfortunate accident.

"You're an honest-looking young man. How's about you run a little errand for me, son?" my dad asks. I nod so forcefully blood rushes to my ears. He called me "son"! I would run to Steinberg's wearing a corset for this guy! "Great! Although the corset is not necessary." He smiles, grabs both my shoulders, and looks me right in the eye.

"I need you to go to Mulcrone's and get a crate of dried beef. Can you handle that?" Of course I can. I don't want my dad to think I can't handle something as minor as a crate of dried beef.

"I thought so," he says, ruffling my hair. I flinch a little, thinking about how he smacked poor Joey, but I also can't help smiling. My dad grins back. "You'd make a dad proud," he says, and my breath catches a little.

Does he know I'm his son? I wait to see if he wants to continue, but he just waves a hand. "Okay, go on now. And if they ask who sent you, tell them Captain Slater." He smiles, his eyes flat and steely. "They'll know who you're talking about."

I skedaddle toward town, half excited, half nervous, half feeling like I still need to use the privy, which I know equals three halves, but that's how many feelings I'm having.

Of all people, Mrs. Law, Cuddy's grandmother, is leaving the store as I enter. I duck my head, hoping she doesn't see me, but no such luck.

"Mr. Slater," she says crisply. I raise my eyes to hers. "Shouldn't you be in school?" I nod because technically, yes, I should be. But I don't want to start a discussion with this woman about how school is stunting my ability to earn money for my mama and avoid a future as Mr. Crutchley's stepson.

"Archibald Crutchley?" Mrs. Law asks, eyebrow raised. I nod. "Hmm," she says. "He would be a good match for your mother. And for you."

Well, he looks happy enough.

I tip my cap to her and head inside, hopefully a strong enough hint this conversation is over, but her skeletal fingers clutch my arm. "And don't forget to pick up Cuddy," she warns. "You may want to ruin your own life by skipping an education and

THE JOLLY TRAMP

becoming a vagrant, but you will not forgo the care of my grandson."

She releases my arm and straightens her hair. "For some reason, the boy thinks the sun rises and sets on you. Please don't disappoint him." And with a further sharp look over the rims of her spectacles, she trots down the stairs to a waiting carriage.

I sigh. I don't want to disappoint Cuddy, but it's not really my fault he likes me so much. A lot of people like me. There's Cuddy. And Mama. And Stinky Pete. And . . . and . . . probably a lot of other people who haven't met me yet.

Also, the sun does happen to rise and set on me. It's just what it does. It's science.

"You here for the mail, Stan?" Mr. Mulcrone asks as I approach the counter. "Little early today. Aren't you supposed to be in school, young man?" He's a friendly kind of guy, so even though his words sound disapproving, he's not going to turn me in to Mama or anything.

"Um, actually, Mr. Mulcrone, I've been asked to pick up a crate of dried beef."

He rests his arms on the counter and leans in. "And who's this for?" he asks. "This on your mom's account or the Carlisles'?" He pulls out his ledger.

"Neither," I answer. "It's for my da—for Captain Slater, sir." Simply saying his name makes me feel proud.

But it also seems to make other people feel, well, something else entirely. Three grown men start coughing, a lady utters, "Oh, my," and Mr. Mulcrone, usually so talkative, immediately puts away his ledger, pinches his lips, and nods to a boy to get the crate.

"Here," he says, thrusting it at me like it holds Mr. Glashaw's glass eye and Granny's dentures, and while we're at it, we could throw in some cod liver oil, too. All things I would avoid like the plague if possible.

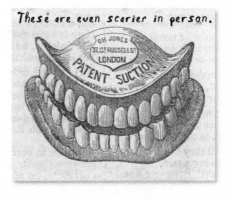

These are even scarier in person.

I scoot the box toward me. It's heavy, but I am strong. And manly.

"Oof!" I say, nearly dropping it. "Will you be sending a bill, Mr. Mulcrone?" I ask. I'm pretty sure my dad would appreciate this professional touch.

Mr. Mulcrone just shakes his head and shoos me out the door. "It's fine. Fine," he says crisply. But his face, along with all the others in the store, looks less like he's fine and more

as if he's bitten into an apple and found a worm.

"But, Stan," he adds, as if he just remembered something. "Well . . ."

Well what? Hurry up! This crate is heavy!

His eyelids droop like his mustache, making him look like a friendly rag doll. "I just want you to be careful. A man is known by the company he keeps," he says.

I nod, but I have no idea what he's talking about. I don't have a company. I don't like it when company comes over because then I have to wear clean trousers and sit up straight and watch how much I eat, and I end up uncomfortable and hungry and generally ill-tempered. So I am not keeping any company, that's for sure.

I lug the crate out the door and wonder what exactly just happened in that store. Why did people gasp when I said my dad's name? And why did he get this crate of beef for free?

I pause to catch my breath. This thing is heavy, but I don't want my dad to think I can't handle it, so I muster all my strength, grimace through the pain, and meander my way toward the *Wanderer* like I know what I'm doing.

I don't have any idea what I'm doing. And with my dad watching me, I realize this more than ever. Also, this crate is heavy and is making me walk like a drunken sailor.

My dad snickers when he sees me. "You been hittin' the

bottle?" he jokes as he takes the crate. I feel like I no longer weigh anything and am floating off into the air. "They charge you?"

I shake my head no, still afraid to say anything out loud in case my voice squeaks or I say something stupid.

I don't want my dad to think I'm stupid.

I'm a whiz at not being stupid, I don't mind saying. Although don't ask Geri about that. Or Mad Madge. Or Granny. You can ask Cuddy, however. He knows the truth.

"Good thing they didn't charge you!" My dad looks as pleased as a boy with a pet monkey.

This is exactly what I imagine doing with a pet monkey.

Except fighting each other. I wouldn't make them fight.

He gives the crate to a deckhand, reaches into his pocket, and throws something my way. "Thanks, kid," he says. "You were a big help. Come back. I'll have more work for you."

I snatch it out of the air. It's a quarter! That little errand earned me a twenty-five-cent piece. Between this job and watching Cuddy, I will be rich! Mama won't have to marry Mr. Crutchley, and we'll be able to fix up the boardinghouse.

And we can send Granny back to Chicago with Geri. I'll pay for the tickets myself.

"Thanks!" I say, but my dad is nowhere to be found, evaporated like this morning's fog.

I whistle my way down the dock, thinking my rich man's thoughts about new bicycles and maybe a fur coat for Mama and a jackknife for me.

"Stan! Ovah heah!" I certainly know that voice. There's Sheriff Dolan leaning against the depot building. "Whatcha doin' down theah?" he asks, nodding toward the boats. His thick Boston accent makes him seem even more official than the star pinned to his chest.

"Um, helping out?"

"And who was yah helping out?" he asks through the toothpick dangling from his mouth. He throws it to the ground without taking his eyes off me.

"Um." I look over my shoulder nervously. "Um, just one of the captains. I'm done now," I reassure him, because Sheriff Dolan looks suspicious.

"Naht that Cap'n Slater, was it?" His eyes are slivers.

I think for a minute, then shake my head no.

"Good. Stay away from that fellah, yah heah me, son?"

I nod. What is it with everyone calling me "son"?

"Stan!"

And what is it with everyone calling my name? It's such a burden being so popular.

"Whatcha up to, man?" Stinky Pete strolls up and claps me on the back. I don't really feel like looking him in the face, his ruddy, smiley Stinky Pete face. I feel like the time I switched Granny's bar of soap with a hunk of lard, which was fine until she decided I needed a good scrubbing behind the ears. I think it's obvious what happened next.

Let's just say I ended up a bit slippery and the cats loved me.

Granny said I got my just deserts for that prank. Frankly, I thought she was talking about desserts, so understandably I felt a little let down.

Which is exactly how I feel now. Let down. And like I might have let someone else down.

I was delicious.

He was delicious.

"What was Sheriff Dolan saying to you?" Stinky Pete asks. He rests his elbow on my head, forcing my cap over my eye. I straighten it up and back away. For some reason his usual friendly self annoys me.

"Oh, you know. Stuff."

Stinky Pete looks confused. Or befuddled, like a pan of water just starting to simmer. "Aren't you supposed to be in school?" he asks, his head slightly tilted, his arms crossed.

"Um. Maybe." I can't lie to that guy. He's too, well, too nice. And I mean that in a bad way. In a way that even if you were the Pope of England and had never said a swearword or thought a bad thought, you'd still feel like you weren't quite good enough standing next to Stinky Pete.

The queen is here.

England, France. Where the queen lives.

I'm a whiz at popes. And geography, I don't mind saying. I know right where the Catholic Church is. And Uncle Erick sent me a postcard from England once.

"Let me escort you back to school," Stinky Pete says. "I'm going that way anyway." Which is not at all true since the Martel Furnace Company is in the opposite direction.

Stinky Pete yammers on

about going to the World's Fair in Chicago a couple of years ago, and how he happened to still be in town the day the mayor was shot two days before the fair closed. And how a man named Nicholas Dresser demonstrated all sorts of uses of electricity.

I imagine he looks a little like this.

"Tesla. Nikola Tesla, Stan. Remember that name. He's going to be known forever in history books."

But once again, all Stinky Pete's yammering does is remind me how little I've done in my almost twelve years of life, how little I've seen of the world, how ordinarily ordinary I am.

Stinky Pete stops. He's

But I was wrong. He actually looks like this.

I am famous. And very good-looking.

288 Fifth Aveni

always about a good four steps ahead of me, so I almost run into him. Both of his hands brace my shoulders, and I look up before I have a chance to think.

"If you've never heard anything I've said before, Stan, listen to me now. You don't need to prove anything to anyone to be worth your weight in gold. You, my man, are the least ordinary person I know." He lets out a little laugh. "And one of my favorite people in the entire world."

My throat catches. I want to believe him, but just going to school and watching over a seven-year-old is not going to get a new roof on the boardinghouse. It's not even enough to buy a carpet sweeper that will save my poor, aching back.

Is it too much to ask?
My back needs saving!

"Stan, I don't think I've ever seen you lift a finger to pick lint off the carpet, let alone sweep it," Stinky Pete says. His arm drapes lightly across my back as he steers me toward the school.

But I still have that lump in my throat and it might be creeping toward my eyes. I might not need to prove anything to Stinky Pete, but I'm pretty sure my real dad will be a whole lot harder to impress.

Oh! Socks! How exciting!

THE BEST MATERIAL AND
THE BEST WORKMANSHIP
Conduce to the Greatest Durability,
which means in the case of stockings,—what is appreciated by the
busy or tired housewife,—
THE LEAST DARNING.
THE *Shawknit* STOCKINGS
TRADE MARK.
are made of the *Best Yarns,* on the *Best Machinery,* and by the *Best
Skilled Labor.*
SHAW STOCKING CO., LOWELL, MASS.
☞ SEND FOR DESCRIPTIVE PRICE-LIST.

CHAPTER 19

You didn't ask me about school today, Stan. No, you didn't. Don't you want to know how my day went, Stan? Mother always asks Father about his day. Don't you think you should ask about my day?"

I'm actually not sure I should ask Cuddy about his day. For one thing, we're not married. For another, what interesting thing could have happened to Cuddy today? Yesterday he was excited because he got new socks. The day before he went on and on about some worm that got stuck to his shoe. I can appreciate an overactive imagination, but I've got too many other things on my mind.

"Perhaps today you should take the time to see the

surprise Cuddy has been dying to show you," Geri whispers. I start to inform her of all the times I've tried to see his surprise but have been foiled in the process, but I can't get a word in edgewise. She sounds like she's giving a sermon. Like the sermon Reverend Elliot gave last week about doing something unto others? Or having other people do something to you?

I'm not quite sure because I might have been picking a scab while he was talking.

He talks a lot.

"Maybe I remind you of Reverend Elliot because you have a guilty conscience, Stan," Geri says. "You could learn something from those sermons." She's still whispering. Probably because she doesn't want Cuddy to hear us and get upset. Or ask what a guilty conscience is.

"What is a guilty conscience?" Cuddy asks. He holds my hand and peers up at me, his face its usual dirty and sticky self. I adjust his crooked cap and smile at him.

I can't help smiling at that kid. He grins back. I notice his two front teeth are missing. When did that happen?

"You know that feeling when you do something you shouldn't?" Geri asks Cuddy, but she's looking directly at me. Cuddy nods.

"I sure do. I sure do know that feeling, Miss Geri," he says sadly. "One time I ate the last cookie right after Mother said not to or it would spoil my dinner. And do you know what, Miss Geri?" He doesn't wait for Geri to answer. "It sure did spoil my dinner, but not because I was full of cookie and couldn't eat. No, because I had done something Mother asked me not to do, that's why. I couldn't even eat my dinner, and it was my favorite—pot roast with potatoes and gravy."

My stomach rumbles.

"Have you ever felt that way, Miss Geri? Have you? I'd ask Stan, but I know he could never have a guilty conscience, could you, Stan?"

I shake my head no, even though I sure have had that feeling. And I've had it more lately than ever before.

"C'mon, Cuddy," Geri says, reaching for his other hand. "Let's get you home."

I have a sick feeling in my gut as I do it, but I let go of Cuddy's hand. I know it's not right, but it's like I can't control my brain, like I'm a buggy and someone else has taken over the driving.

"Hey, thanks, Geri!" I say. Both she and Cuddy look at me, confused. "I've got, uh, a couple errands to run," I add.

Geri's eyebrows knit together, like thunderclouds quickly forming over the lake.

Cuddy looks at me like I've taken his cap and thrown it in a tree and he has no idea why.

I don't have any idea why, either. But I can't help it.

"But, Stan," he starts. "We were going to look at my surprise. . . ."

I cup my hand around my ear while breaking into a jog. "What? What was that, Cuddy? I will see you in the morning, son!" I point a finger at him, wink, and dart in the opposite direction. Geri's glare cuts through the air, as harsh as a north wind.

But I'll deal with her and my conscience later, because right now my dad is calling me. Not with his words, exactly. Well, not with his words at all, but with his simply being here, in this town at the same time as me.

And while on one hand it doesn't make me feel good at all to act this way, on the other hand, I don't have a choice. It's like a magnet and steel. Me and bacon. Sailors and tattoos. Geri and deadly diseases. Mad Madge and bad news. Some things, and some people, just belong together.

Like me and my dad.

Me with all my tattoos. After years at sea.

My dog. Every sailor should have a dog.

CHAPTER 20

I wander down the docks. It's practically my second home now, I'm here so often, running an errand or two for my dad. Some of the guys nod at me or tip their caps. I'm one of them. I'm thinking about getting a tattoo soon. And maybe I'll start smoking cigars. And I'm going to start spitting more.

I spit on the planks. It's a good feeling. I'm a whiz at spitting, I don't mind saying. Although I'm not such a whiz at aiming because the spit landed on my shoe. I'm going to need more practice.

"Boy!" I hear my dad holler. I may have meandered my way near the *Wanderer*. I may have been hoping my dad might be there. I may have been right.

"C'mere!" he says, waving me over. I point to myself in a surprised *Who? Me?* kind of way, and my dad chuckles and jogs down the docks to throw his heavy arm around me. He laughs as he guides me toward the ship. His laugh is like ice skimming a puddle, thin and sharp.

"I was just telling the fellows what a great job you've been doing." Five guys gather around barrels near the gangplank. They don't look very impressed. Two of them look like they could use some sleep, another has his hat over his eyes and is snoring, the fourth guy stares at me blankly while tugging on his cigarette, and Joey stands at attention, his eyes never leaving my dad. He looks as jumpy as a popcorn kernel in a vat of hot oil.

My dad thumps my back, making me stumble. "Ha! You're right! Joey is about as jumpy as a cheating husband in a room full of ex-wives. Ha! Am I right?" He slugs Joey, who smiles slightly and rubs his arm.

One of the guys rumples Joey's hair and grins. I think if you took all the men's teeth and put them together, they'd make one nice set; sailing must be hard on a person's dental

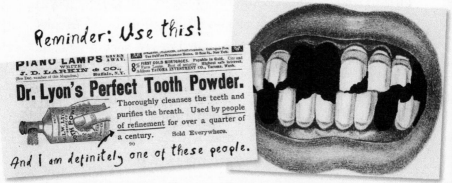

Reminder: Use this!

PIANO LAMPS GIVEN AWAY. WHITE J. D. LARKIN & CO., Buffalo, N.Y. (See Dec. number of this Magazine.)

SPEAKERS, DIALOGUES, ENTERTAINMENTS. Catalogue Free THE DeWitt Publishing House, 33 Rose St., New York.

8% FIRST GOLD MORTGAGES. Payable in Gold. City and Farm Loans. Best of security. Highest safe interest. Address TACOMA INVESTMENT CO., Tacoma, Wash.

Dr. Lyon's Perfect Tooth Powder.
Thoroughly cleanses the teeth and purifies the breath. Used by people of refinement for over a quarter of a century. Sold Everywhere.
90

And I am definitely one of these people.

Or your teeth may end up like this!

hygiene. I make a note to bring my tooth powder when I take up the seafaring life.

"So, as I was saying, this is the guy who got us an entire crate of dried beef for nothin' down at Mulcrone's. Not to mention sundry items from Steinberg's, eh?" He elbows me so hard I stumble again. I need to work on my sea legs if I'm going to hang around this crew.

"The boy said that once he said the order was for me, they just gave him the stuff, right, son?" I nod and smile. One of the guys takes a swig from a brown bottle. Another one takes a drink from a jug. He hands it to Joey, but my dad swipes it and takes a long draw.

"Care for some?" he asks me. I'm tempted. I don't want to let him or the other guys down, and I want to feel like part of the group, even though I don't yet have any tattoos and I have more teeth than all of these guys put together. I reach out, but just as I do my dad's face changes.

All the blood drains, his arm drops, and he straightens up like he's four years old and his mother is coming after him with a switch because he may or may not have dressed the cat in his cousin's finest bonnet.

Not that I know anything about that. Also, that bonnet looked better on the cat than on Geri, I don't mind saying.

THE SWEET SINGER

I swing around to see what might have made my dad react so strangely.

Then I wish I hadn't, because who should I see striding down the merchandise dock like she's marching off to war but Mama. And she's madder than a wet hen sitting on a cold egg.

My dad hands off the jug to one of the guys, all of whom have snapped to attention, mainly out of curiosity, I think. I can't imagine many people cause this kind of reaction in the good captain.

It *is* impressive, my little mama standing up to this motley crew.

Mama stops abruptly in front of my dad. All the fellows have removed their caps and are knotting them in their hands. Except for my dad. His shoulders shiver like he's shedding rain from his back as he steps up to Mama, a smile snaking its way up his bristly cheeks.

"Well, Alice!" he says, shaking his head in wonder. "You look lovely." His voice sounds like pebbles rolling around in my hand, waiting to be flung at something.

But Mama is having none of it. She stands like a string dangles her from heaven and stares at my father like no one I've yet seen. And I realize why.

She's not afraid of him.

But he's right. She does look pretty. Even wearing an apron speckled with grease and a smudge of flour under her right eye, her cheeks are flushed and her skin is like the alabaster doll Geri uses for her science experiments.

The spark in her eye makes me want to take a step back, however.

"Alice, Alice, Alice," my dad says, approaching her with his arms wide. She sticks a hand in his face.

"Stay away from my son." She makes each word sound like a threat.

My dad startles, his eyes darting between Mama and me, then landing on me with a thud. His mouth drops and his head bobbles slightly, until he nods slowly, like he's seeing me for the first time.

I stop breathing. Mama's arm falls to her side like she's a knight throwing down a gauntlet.

But my dad, my strong hero of a dad, broadens his shoulders quickly and switches his gaze toward Mama. "You mean to tell me, Alice," he says, "that this boy here—this young *man*, I should say—is my *son*?" His tone makes it sound like a question, but he knows the answer. I know he knows the answer. And I think he might like the answer.

Mama swallows. Slowly, like her throat hurts. And nods. Slowly.

"You don't say!" he says, looking at me with a half smile. He cocks his head and one eyebrow. "He sure does favor your brothers, don't he?"

"You left, Arthur. Remember? You left," Mama says quietly. But it's her quiet voice that sounds like her yelling voice, only much scarier.

I reach over and squeeze her hand. Twice. Because I don't want her to ruin this for me.

"Yup. I did. I did leave," my dad says agreeably. "But I didn't know what a fine fellow I'd be leaving, now, did I?"

My insides feel happy and scared, like I'm inhaling bubbles and they're jumping around in my belly. I can't help grinning into my dad's smiling face, the face that makes me think I'm looking in a mirror, we look so much alike. Except for the fact that his eyes are blue and mine are brown. And he's got lots of bristly whiskers and I only have whiskers if I draw them on with a fountain pen. Also, his jaw is square and his nose is pointy. But other than that, we could be twins.

"And you can't keep a man from his son, can you, Alice?" My dad directs the question toward Mama, but he's looking right at me.

I know Mama is not pleased. Her arms hang at her sides, the steam from her anger floating off her like sighs. When I look at her, I feel a little like a kite with no wind.

"Arthur, he has to go to school. He has missed three days this week, and I know it's because he's been down here with you," she says.

"Oh, yes. Oh, school is important," my dad reassures her.

She takes a deep breath and grabs my hand. My dad squeezes my shoulder one more time and winks.

We both know school isn't important, but we also know not to worry the little lady about it.

"Come see me tomorrow, son," he says. Did he just emphasize the word *son*?

"*After* school," my mother reminds both of us. We nod in agreement. "You have your job with the Carlisle family," she says sternly. "Mrs. Carlisle still can't get around that well, and I don't want to remind her why that is the case."

She hauls me down the dock, mumbling about how keeping a boy from his father is not a good idea. As if she's trying to convince herself.

She doesn't have to convince me. I turn around for one last look. My dad salutes me, then rubs his hands together like they're cold.

It all leaves me feeling like I'm a rope in a tug-of-war contest. The last time I participated in such a battle, Conrad McAllister pulled the rope so hard and so fast I ended up dragged through the mud and had dirt in my teeth for two days.

I sure hope this doesn't end up the same way.

Stop watching me, people!

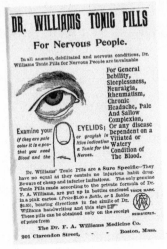

Well, I wouldn't be so nervous if everyone would just leave me alone.

CHAPTER 21

Today Miss Wenzel was her usual ornery self. She rarely let me out of her sight from the minute I dropped Cuddy at his classroom until now, when she takes Cuddy's hand and puts it directly into mine.

"Now, Stanley," she says, "mind Cuddy and get him home in a timely fashion. And should you need to run errands, please be sure to do them like a responsible young man and valuable member of this society." She pinches both of my cheeks and tilts my head up. "And your mother says to stay away from the docks." Then she pushes both of us toward the door.

"Thanks, Missus Wenzel! Thank you!" Cuddy hollers,

skipping outside. Here we find Geri, leaning against the building and eating some bacon that's probably been in her pocket all day.

I'm hungry. I would like some bacon.

Geri hands a slice to Cuddy, who grabs it greedily. "Then maybe you shouldn't have eaten all of yours at lunch," she says.

"'Ere, Sthtan! Dew can had sthom of mine," Cuddy says. He obviously has stuffed the entire piece into his mouth. Someone needs to teach that boy some manners.

"Where are you all going?" Madge asks, sliding in next to Geri.

"What's with all the questions?" I hiss. And why is everyone always following me?

"All good journalists ask questions, Stan," Geri says huffily. "Also, we're not supposed to let you go down to the docks."

I stop abruptly and stamp my foot with a snort. "I am not some baby who needs to be followed or watched all the time. Leave me alone!"

Cuddy stops chewing long enough to stare at me. Geri sighs. Madge pulls out a pencil and a pad of paper and starts taking notes.

I doubt Nellie Bly herself asked so many questions.

Why do you say that?

Fine. I get it. I'm acting like a baby who needs to be followed or watched all the time.

I do have a list of errands to run for Mrs. Carlisle, but it's the usual: soap, a razor for Mr. Carlisle, the mail.

Geri and Madge and Cuddy never leave my side. And the folks at the stores seem a bit less talkative than usual. Oh, sure, they still chat with Cuddy because most people have no choice, but I no longer hear a friendly "Hello, Stan!" or "What can I do for you, son?" No, now all the storekeepers and staff see me, barely nod, hand me my merchandise or mail, don't make eye contact, and turn the other way.

It all started on the first day I ran that errand for my dad. Do they know who my dad is? Is that why they're acting this way? Is that why they're treating me so special?

"Pfft," Madge snorts. Or maybe it's Geri. Or both of them. It's not Cuddy because he's over at a puddle stirring a leaf into the mud with a stick.

"You would make a lousy journalist, I'll tell you what," Madge says. "They're all treating you so *special* because they're afraid of what your dad might do to them if they don't."

"How do you know?" I ask.

"As I keep telling you, I'm a journalist. My eyes and ears are always open. I have my finger on the pulse of this town," Madge says.

"Also, Granny found out your father has been warning all the shopkeepers to be extra respectful to his son, Stan, or they'd have to answer to him," Geri adds.

"He did?" I ask. I'm amazed. He did that for me?

"That's not a good thing," Geri says. "All these people look out for you on a day-to-day basis. They know your family, ask about your health, keep an eye on Cuddy when you're distracted by, oh, anything. They are the people who have been here for you when your dad has not. And now they're scared of you, Stan."

That's certainly not a good thing, and I'm kind of sorry about that, but to have my very own father looking out for me is a feeling I'm not used to. He might seem gruff. He might be rough and tumble and drive a hard bargain. But he can't be all bad, right? Mama married him, and she wouldn't have married some good-for-nothing bum. And he must really be glad he's my father if he took the trouble to talk to all the shopkeepers about me.

"Well, that's one way to look at it," Geri says in a voice that means she's looking at it in a completely different way.

I gather up Cuddy and his stick and aim them both toward our next stop but can't help glancing down the dock. Sure enough, leaning against the depot is my dad, smoking a cigarette. He salutes as we pass.

"Stop by when you're done with errands, son!" he yells.

I wave back, my heart beating so fast I can hear it in my ears.

"Brrr," Madge says, shaking her body from head to toe. "That man makes my flesh crawl."

"What? What can you possibly mean?" I ask.

Madge and Geri exchange a glance. Geri shakes her head almost unnoticeably. Except I notice.

I'm a whiz at noticing things, I don't mind saying.

"Stan! Watch out for that puddle," Cuddy says, skirting it himself.

Except for puddles. I'm up to my ankles in cold water. Apparently I don't always notice puddles.

"At least it's just a puddle, right, Stan? And not a lake, right?"

I stomp my feet and listen to Cuddy recite all the bodies of freshwater in the world, starting with the Great Lakes.

"There's Lake Michigan, Stan, and Lake Huron, and . . ." But as we get farther from the docks, all I can think of is how to return there. How can I get rid of these people? How can I just check in with my dad so that he won't forget me? So he'll want to spend more time with me? So he'll want to stay here in St. Ignace? Or so if he does leave, he'll come back?

"Um, Madge and Geri, I've got it from here. I know you two have some, um, girl stuff you probably want to get to." These are two of the least girlie girls I've ever met, but doesn't every girl have girl stuff to do?

They wash clothes for their menfolk.

And they're happy doing it!

"How long have you known me?" Geri asks.

I want to say "Too long," but I know better. Cuddy wiggles his eyebrows at me. He knows me. And he knows better, too.

Fortunately, Geri doesn't wait for me to trip on my words. "We are hardly frivolous girls with nothing to do. But it just so happens Madge and I have a project we've been working on"—they share a glance—"and since we can see Cuddy's house from here, I think it might be okay to leave you by yourself for the few minutes it should take to drop him off and come right home."

Madge nods, and the two of them head to the boarding-house.

"But don't you dare go down to the docks," Geri warns. "Because I will tell your mama, don't think I won't."

And then there's just Cuddy and me.

"And there's Lake Baikal, Stan. Ever hear of that lake, huh? I bet you haven't. Because it's in Russia, Stan. That's way far away. Farther than Mackinac Island."

I have heard of Russia, of course. And I can see Mackinac Island from where I'm standing right now, at the bottom of Cuddy's steps, so I'm pretty sure I know Russia is farther away than Mackinac Island, but who am I to tell Cuddy this? Plus, who am I to interrupt the guy? That's about as impossible as pushing a wet noodle up a hill.

"Well, I know about it, Stan, because my uncle Cuthbert—you know, the guy I was named for?—he was working on the Trans-Siberian Railway and wrote me a letter telling me about this huge freshwater lake. And Father says it's all true. He acted surprised, but he said what Uncle Cuthbert wrote was all true."

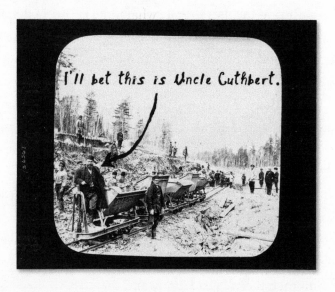

I'll bet this is Uncle Cuthbert.

He keeps talking as I push open the door to his house, nodding along but thinking my own thoughts. I'm still worried about money. About my dad. About Mad Madge and

Geri and why they looked so suspicious. About my dad again. For some reason, the guy I know the least is the one I think about the most.

"Very well." Mrs. Law stops me before I can step foot in the foyer. "Your work is done for the day." She glances at my muddy shoes, her lips pinched like she just bit into a lemon. She hands me a twenty-five-cent piece and shuts the door.

Cuddy is probably still listing bodies of water, not yet aware I'm stuck outside. I hear him knock on the window, his face pressed against the glass, his eyes buggy and his tongue halfway out his mouth. I laugh and wave until Mrs. Law pulls him by the collar, away from my view.

Poor bugger. I know exactly what it's like to have a granny with no sense of humor.

This is a train.

This is a boat.

CHAPTER 22

I saunter toward town. Leisurely. Casually. Like I haven't got a care in the world.

I have lots of cares in this world. Mama. The boardinghouse. Mr. Crutchley. Money. Geri. Cuddy. Mad Madge and her one-man gang, although she no longer seems so mad, and I can't remember the last time I ran into Nincompoop.

And, most of all, my dad, who is still at the depot, smoking a cigarette. I know I'm not allowed on the docks, at least if you ask Mama, but the depot is not the dock, really. It's where the trains come in, not the boats, and we all know trains and boats are two entirely different things. Just like docks and depots. So if I happen to meander near the depot and my dad happens to see me and want to talk, it would be rude not to.

"Hey, son!" my dad yells. He sounds like fog and thunder and waves crashing against the wharf. "Come on over here!" he orders. And who am I to say no? I've been taught to respect my elders, and I'm pretty sure that must include my dad.

"How was your day at school?" he says with a wink. He elbows the guy next to him, one of the men I recognize from the *Wanderer*. "Not that any man needs school, eh, Jeb?" He elbows his friend again. "None of that ed-u-ma-cation for us real men, eh?" He winks at me again, laying his meaty hand on my shoulder.

For some reason I remember Stinky Pete saying something like "He who opens a school door closes a prison."

"Yep. I did. It's a Victor Hugo quote, can't take credit for it myself," says someone behind me. Obviously it's Stinky Pete. I can tell by his twinkly voice. Except right now it doesn't sound so twinkly, and when I look up at his ruddy face, he doesn't look twinkly, either.

He looks like Granny did

last time I stole a plate of food to take to the kittens. And Eugene.

He looks mad.

He's also not looking at me.

"I don't think I've met you fellows," Stinky Pete says.

My dad thrusts out an arm to shake hands; Jeb leans against the depot building, one leg bent like the number four. He spits something brown and thick into the dirt at Stinky Pete's feet.

Stinky Pete glances at the spit and then at Jeb. "And I don't think I need to meet you," he says, placing a hand on my back. His hand is warm through my coat as he aims me toward Main Street.

I keep an eye on my dad as we turn.

"Hey!" my dad says. He sounds like a freshly sharpened razor when he yells. "That's my son." My eyes water and my throat thickens when I hear him call me "son." "You don't have the right to take him away from me! You hear me? I've got some work for him. Make him a man, not some namby-pamby professor."

Jeb snorts.

Stinky Pete's grip tenses and his jaw tightens, but I can't help glancing at my dad and Jeb. Jeb smiles a crooked smile, and my dad stands straight and squared, like a high-strung racehorse shut in a starting box. He looks so threatening I feel like I should warn Stinky Pete, but I don't really know what I'm warning him about. Or if I'm selling out my dad if I do.

Stinky Pete guides us toward the boardinghouse. "You don't have to warn me about Arthur Slater, Stan," he says. "I know exactly what kind of man he is."

I nod. I might know exactly what kind of man he is, too. And even though I'm not so sure I like him, I really want him to like me.

CHAPTER 23

L ying in my bed, in the dark, I imagine the entire thing. My future. Unless I die of dysentery first.

Geri told me I have it. Granny said I just have a stomachache and gave me some cod liver oil, which did nothing but make me burp fish.

I still have a stomachache, so I'm pretty sure Geri is right.

When Stinky Pete and I got home, all I could think about was that my dad had work for me. Work. Work means money, and money means saving Mama and me from the unsavory Mr. Archibald Crutchley.

"I think your mama might need to be saved from *you*," Geri said. She was eavesdropping again. "It's not eavesdropping when we're sitting right next to each other on the sofa and you're talking out loud." Geri snorted.

But I'm pretty sure it was a private conversation.

And why would my mama need to be saved from me?

"Well, because all of your recent shenanigans are making her sick with worry, can't you see that? Everything your mother does is so you will have a better life. But instead of making it easier for her, you do things like forget Cuddy after school or run down to the docks to see your no-good father, not to mention the irresponsible behavior that started all this in the first place," Geri said as she jotted notes from her medical textbook.

The one she stole from Dr. McKinnon.

Geri threw down her fountain pen. "I didn't steal it, Stan! I don't steal things! It's not in my nature to take things that aren't mine," she said pointedly. She really did point at me. Her finger almost poked out my eye.

"What do you mean?" I was insulted. Was she implying I steal things?

"I'm not *implying* anything. I'm just saying I'm starting to think the apple doesn't fall far from the tree." Her eyes glared, and her cheeks flushed.

"What's *that* supposed to mean?" I didn't even understand that statement. Where else would apples fall? It's not like they have legs or anything. Or wings.

"It's a saying, Stan. It means maybe you're not so different from your dad." But she said it like it's a bad thing.

Is it a bad thing to be like your dad?

"It is when your dad is a liar and a thief! And scares people into giving him things," Geri said. Then she scooped up her book and fountain pen and paper and stormed off to her room.

"At least my parents want me!" I yelled. "They didn't ship me off somewhere with Granny and then forget to make arrangements for me to come home!"

Geri's door flew open so fast I'm pretty sure the hinges almost caught fire. "For your information," she said, "my parents have sent a train ticket for my return. But they care about my health, and we all know the poor air quality in Chicago is not good for my lungs." Then she slammed the door.

And now I'm lying here. Thinking about what she said.

Mama breathes evenly and slowly, and I time my breath with hers. I stare at the ceiling. Eugene murmurs to the cats behind the house, and a train hoots in the distance.

Would Mama be better off without me? Am I a liar? A thief? Am I like my dad? And is it really so bad to be a rich, smart, infamous criminal?

I'm not going to fall back to sleep, no matter what I try. I pull out my scrapbook, some magazines, and scissors—it's the best way I know to forget my troubles, or figure them out.

The full moon gives just enough light, and I work quietly so as not to wake Mama.

You have probably heard of my amazing dental escapades.

Dear Stan,

It's true. I'm a criminal. People always act like that's a bad thing, but it's not really my fault. I have an awful girl cousin—Scary Mary—who never stops diagnosing me with deadly diseases. I am constantly dying, and it is more than one soul can bear. Now I have consumption and am forced to live a life of crime.

Not horrible crime. More like self-defense. Like the time this guy was cheating at cards—I might have had to stab him a little bit. Or the time that other guy shot at me and I had to shoot back. Actually, that may have happened a lot of times, but it's not my fault they didn't know I'm an expert marksman.

I also saved Wyatt Earp's life, so that should count for something, him being a lawman and all. And I am a dentist, fluent in Latin, have impeccable manners, and I play the piano like, well, like a really, really good piano player.

I also dress really nice.

So see! It's not all bad being a criminal. In fact, I'd say it's not bad at all!

Yours in crime,
Doc Holliday

FREDERICK WARDES's
SUPER PRODUCTION

But
with
a gun.

FREDERICK WARDE
IN
ROBIN HOOD

RUNNYMEDE

Dear Stan,

Some people consider me a criminal, but that's such a harsh word, don't you think? I prefer to consider myself a modern-day Robin Hood; you know, take from the rich and give to the poor? That's exactly what robbing banks is—taking money from the rich bankers in order to make sure people like your mama have enough money to put a roof over your heads and don't have to marry someone with the absolutely atrocious name of Archibald Crutchley.

Also, I read my Bible every day and never curse.

Is it my fault that some folks are greedy and don't want to share? If they are rich enough to take a train or stagecoach across this country of ours, they should share. And if that so-called Pinkerton detective agency can't stop us, perhaps it's because we are doing good work and the good Lord himself is watching out for us.

Also, it might be my brother Frank's fault. He's always been a bad influence.

Sharing is caring!
Jesse James

Gun.

Ignore
the gun.

Me—model citizen

Frank. See what a bad influence he is?

Dear Stan,

You may have heard of me. William the Child? Bill the Juvenile? Willy the Youngster? No?

How about Billy the Kid? Huh? Have you heard that name? Really, how scary or evil or threatening can someone with the last name of The Kid actually be?

Exactly.

I am not scary, evil, or threatening.

Sure, I may rustle some cattle or horses from time to time, but I prefer to think of it as rescuing these poor animals from lives of unending boredom out on the plains, a place so dull that even whoever named it thought it was plain. So there you have it.

And, yes, I have been accused of counterfeiting some dollar bills, but that was simply a silly misunderstanding. My friends and I are really good

artists. One day we drew dollar signs on some paper, those papers got mixed up with some real money, and then we accidentally spent some of the fake money. Happens all the time.

Is it our fault we draw really well? Is drawing a crime?

Oh. And the stories you may have heard about my escapes from jail? Well, when you cage a man, even a man with the name of a kid, it's human nature to want to escape. I certainly wasn't trying to avoid jail time or anything like that.

Even though I was wrongly accused.

So you can see I'm less like a criminal and more like a magician animal-rescuer artist. And my talents are not being appreciated.

Yours in being underappreciated.

Billy the Kid

Billy the Kid

HORSTON

MASTER MAGICIAN

AND HIS PETS

Thanks for rescuing me, Mr. The Kid.

Don't forget! I'm also an artist!

CHAPTER 24

I must have drifted off and can immediately tell from the light through the window that I've slept in late. The first thing I notice when I wake up is my lucky hat—the one Geri stole, I stole back, and then she stole from me.

It's a very popular hat. And I'm glad to have it returned in one piece.

But I also notice my open scrapbook littered with loose pages stuck here and there all willy-nilly. I definitely did not leave my scrapbook in such a condition, because this is not the way you treat something so valuable.

I put my hat on, but when I start straightening the pages, I become suspicious. These aren't my scrapbook pages.

Someone else has made these and stuck them in my book next to the pages I created last night. Someone has been busy. And that someone has nice, girlie handwriting.

Yes, I am serious. Serious about crime.

Dear Stan,

Don't be such a ninny, trying to convince yourself that criminals can be heroes. Heroes don't go around scaring people, for one thing. Or threatening them.

Oh, it's true, I owe Doc Holliday my life. And I will admit I didn't intend to become a lawman. I spent many years as a buffalo hunter, miner, stagecoach driver, and even a card dealer before taking it upon myself to rid the West of its lawless, wild cowboy ways. You may be familiar with the greatest gunfight in the history of the West. It took place at the O.K. Corral, lasted no more than thirty seconds, and started me on the path toward ensuring the West was safe for women and children alike.

I could have become a criminal, Stan. I could have turned to a life of crime, but I didn't. Because crime does not pay.

Yours in law enforcement,

~~Gert~~ Wyatt Earp

Geri. These letters have Geri written all over them. Especially the part where she accidentally wrote *Geri* and then crossed it out.

I flip to the next page. I have to admit, I am a little curious what other preachy things she's included.

I read the first sentence and all becomes clear:

Mad Madge. And Geri. Is this the project they've been working on? And are they mind readers? How else would they know I would fill my pages with letters from so-called criminals?

> You've been spending too much time reading magazine articles about gangsters and criminals, get-rich-quick schemes, and ways to break out of jail. (By the way, pick up those magazines. Everyone is really tired of sitting on them.)

Oh! Right.

> Criminals should not be considered heroes. Jesse James, for example. He was an armed bank robber, a terrorist on the side of the South during the War of Rebellion, and a murderer. Hardly someone to model your life after.
>
> If Jesse James is Robin Hood, I'm the Grim Reaper and Pope Leo VIII. And you might as well throw in the president of the United States of America, too. Because Jesse James is certainly no hero to the poor. That's a man who thinks only of himself.
>
> Stop thinking only about yourself.
>
> > Yours in thinking about other people,
> > Allan Pinkerton, Private Eye

I'm 99 percent sure these letters aren't real. And I'm 99.9 percent sure Geri and Mad Madge do not bring out the best in each other.

My good friend Wyatt Earp

Bat. Like the flying mammal. You got a problem with that?

Dear Stan,

No matter what you might think when you see my name, I am not a flying mammal.

I am an expert marksman and strict officer of the peace. I have never shot someone out of anger or spite, and I've rarely wasted a bullet, even during my years as a buffalo hunter on the Great Plains.

I've been shot. I've unfortunately taken the lives of others, and I've witnessed the painful death of my brother, Ed, who probably would have lived had a female doctor been available.

All this pain was caused by criminals, Stan. So I became a sheriff and a U.S. marshal and worked alongside my good friend Wyatt Earp to keep this country of ours safe from the very people you seem to idolize.

You may want to rethink your heroes, Stan.

Lawfully yours,
Bat Masterson

Mad Madge and Geri have sullied my scrapbook, but there is no way I'm tricked into thinking any of these guys have actually written me a letter. No, not one of them would be so preachy. Or have such nice handwriting.

They also defaced one of my earlier entries:

Neither one of these girls would know a real hero if he came up and bit her on the nose. Which, I'll admit, would not be a very heroic thing to do, but I wouldn't blame him for doing it.

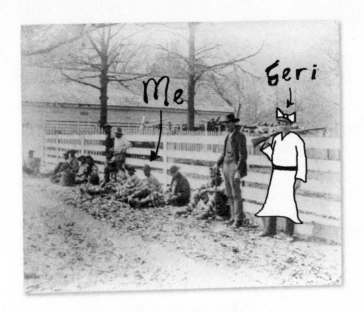

CHAPTER 25

I brought Cuddy to our house after school today. His mother doesn't seem to mind, it's a cheap way to feed him (which means I can keep the money we use for treats along with my weekly twenty-five cents), and if he's distracted, it's very possible I may be able to sneak away for a few minutes.

These people around here have been watching me like a hawk. I feel like a prisoner in my own home.

"Well," Geri says, sitting down on the couch, "if you'd stop running away from your responsibilities every time we look aside for one minute, we wouldn't have to follow you, now, would we?"

Cuddy removes his satchel and plops himself next to Geri. He likes to be as close to her as possible.

"She smells better than you do, Stan," he says, closing his eyes and taking a whiff of the air around Geri.

"If you like the smell of bitterness," I mumble. "And deceit."

"What was that?" Geri asks sharply.

"Um." I think fast. "I said, 'If you like the smell of sweetness and meat.'"

That's some quick thinking right there.

Cuddy nods frantically. "That's exactly what I like, Stan! Sweetness and meat! Bacon, especially."

Geri glares at me but can't help laughing at Cuddy, which makes her a lot less frightening.

"Look what I brought, Stan!" Cuddy says. He reaches into his bag but keeps his eyes on me. They're like saucers, no, dinner plates. Excited dinner plates with eyebrows that move up and down like bouncing parentheses. And his left knee jumps up and down so quickly I'm afraid a leg is going to break off the sofa.

"What?" I ask. "What is it?"

Cuddy reaches in slowly and pulls out . . .

"My *scrapbook*? What are you doing with my scrapbook? That is sacred, Cuddy! No one takes a man's scrapbook," I say, snatching it from his hand.

"Ha! Ha, Stan! This is the surprise I've been trying to show you! It's my very own Mark Twain Self-Pasting Scrapbook! See, Stan? My uncle Cuthbert sent it to me. It's just like yours! Look!"

My heart races as I fall into the chair. My scrapbook isn't valuable, and it probably isn't even interesting to anyone but me, but in that brief moment when I thought Cuddy had taken it, I realized it's priceless.

"Hold on one minute," I say. Geri and Madge have already defaced my scrapbook once, so I know I can't be too careful.

I run upstairs to check on my own, invaluable scrapbook. Sure enough, it's on my bedside table. I grab it and bring it downstairs to remind Cuddy what a real scrapbook is like. A manly scrapbook.

Also, I don't really want it out of my sight.

When I get back to the parlor, Cuddy has his scrapbook open, showing Geri whatever it is he has collected in its pages. Probably old, sticky pieces of candy. Or a picture of some weird animal or a list of the Five Wonders of the World.

I'm a whiz at history, I don't mind saying.

"Obviously you don't mind saying you're a whiz at anything. You're always reminding us. But it's seven, Stan," Geri says.

"It's seven? How can it be seven already? Cuddy, we have to get you home!"

"No, Stan," Geri says. What now? Does she want to button up Cuddy's coat? Remind me to tie his shoes? Give me a map to his house? It's high time she realizes he's my responsibility. She might smell better than I do, but I'm the adult here.

Geri throws her hands to the ceiling. "Fine," she says in that voice that means anything but.

"What about my scrapbook, Stan?" Cuddy asks as I push him out the door.

I dart back in and grab it, because I know what it's like to miss your scrapbook. Like when someone takes it right from under your nose and vandalizes it.

I glare at Geri, grab Cuddy's scrapbook, and stuff it in his bag. Which is still attached to him so he bobs a bit like a cat trying not to fall off a fence.

"Stan." Geri leans toward me like she's going to take the scrapbook, and I jam it farther into the bag.

"What? What now? Are you going to ruin Cuddy's scrapbook, too?" I challenge. She knows I've got her over a barrel, that she's as guilty as any outlaw or swindler or con man or murderer or any bad person in the history of bad people. "And don't touch my scrapbook," I warn.

DELINQUENTS IN CUSTODY OF NEW YORK POLICEMEN.

Geri tilts her head. "Fine, Stan. Go. I'm done trying to help you."

Is that what she's been trying to do? If that's her version of help, I am 92.3 percent sure I'm better off without it.

Finally! Geri is going to leave me alone! But why this makes me feel nervous instead of relieved is more than a bit worrisome. Does she know something I don't?

"She's just special, Stan," Cuddy says wistfully. "She's an angel, she is. So she probably does know things we don't." A little smile plays at his mouth and his eyes look off into the distance. I have to steer him away from any mud puddles because he's obviously not paying attention.

He needs to pay attention.

It's the first time I've noticed the days getting longer. The sun is strong and the air is heavy, like it's clinging to my skin.

No, actually, that's just Cuddy.

"Why are you holding on to me so tightly, Cud?" I ask.

But he just grasps my arm, his little fingers digging in. "I just want to go home, Stan. Can we go home?" he asks. "Now?" I follow his gaze to a pair of men on the street, arguing, a group gathered around them. Some men guide the lady folk away from the ruckus. The rumbling of the crowd makes me feel like I'm outside in a thunderstorm. I completely understand why Cuddy wants to leave.

Cuddy pulls me away from all the uproar. "Whew. That was a close one, Stan. Did you see those men? Did you hear what they were saying? Did you hear one of them say d—" I clamp my hand over Cuddy's mouth. All I need is for Mrs. Law to hear swearwords coming from her dear grandson's lips and I before I could say Jack Sprat, I'd be kicked to the curb and Mama would be heading down the aisle with one Archibald Crutchley.

"Don't use those words, Cuddy. I'm not sure about men who use those words," I say.

He nods, his eyes wide and serious, and I remove my hand, open the door, and usher him in.

The grandfather clock in the hall chimes five times.

"Your clock is off by about two hours, Cuddy," I say,

helping him remove his satchel and laying it on the hall bench.

"No, Stan. Nope. It's five o'clock," Cuddy says. "I can tell because my tummy growls right at five and that means it's time for dinner. That's when I eat, Stan. Five o'clock. And my tummy is never wrong."

"Then why did Geri tell me it was seven?" I wonder out loud.

Cuddy shrugs. "I think she was talking about the Wonders of the World. You said there were five, Stan. There are Seven Wonders of the World. Do you want to hear about them?" he asks eagerly.

It doesn't really matter what I say. Cuddy is going to tell me about them anyway.

"There are the Hanging Gardens of Babylon." Cuddy holds up a finger.

"Time for dinner, Cuthbert." Mrs. Law looms large in the kitchen doorway. She hands me a quarter. "Carry on, Stanley," she says, waving me toward the door.

"Um, maybe next time, Cuddy?" I ruffle his hair. "Right now you have to get to dinner, right?" Cuddy nods. "Okay, buddy! I'll see you

THE SEVEN WONDERS OF THE WORLD.
The Hanging Gardens of Babylon.

I don't see what's so wonderful. It's just a bunch of plants. Nothing is even dangerous. Or exploding.

tomorrow," I say, trying to sound cheery. I slug him in the arm like my dad likes to do to me. Cuddy holds it like it hurts.

"Okay, Stan. Okay. I'll see you tomorrow." His stomach growls as he makes his way to the kitchen.

No. That's my stomach. Except for once I'm not sure I'm hungry—I haven't been down to the docks in more than a day, and I know any minute my dad and his wandering *Wanderer* could up and leave. And once again, I'll be without a father.

I tromp down Cuddy's steps. I've been so busy with Cuddy I haven't even had time to get rich quick. I haven't had time to find any bricks of gold or sell soap or pick Eugene's brain for more ideas. But I *have* made some money. Not fast and not a lot, but when I hand over my twenty-five cents to Mama and she tucks it in her pocket, I feel pretty good.

Stinky Pete always says his heroes are honest men doing honest work. And I guess I see what he means. It's obvious I am his hero.

He also says, "Keep your friends close and your enemies closer," which is the worst thing I've ever heard, so I'm not so sure Stinky Pete should be giving out advice.

As I walk home I realize I have time to spare—two hours more than I thought. Time enough to be my own wanderer without suspicious eyes watching my every move.

Also, I learned something today; there are Seven Wonders of the World, not five. Who knew?

Wait until I tell Geri.

"Tell Geri what?" I jump. Of course it's Madge. She has slithered from an alleyway to join me.

"I didn't 'slither from an alleyway,'" she says. "Honestly, Stan. And I can't for the life of me figure out why you jump like water on a hot griddle every time I show up. I always call your name three or four times before I get to you."

It's like she's insulting my intelligence. Or my lightning-fast reflexes. Or she's implying I don't pay attention.

"Watch the pole!" Madge yells, throwing out an arm.

I almost ran into the pole. It may or may not have been the first time this has happened. But even the most intelligent, attentive, manly men sometimes walk into poles.

It's been proven by science.

"I doubt it, Stan," Madge says. We're approaching State Street, where it seems more folks have gathered since I dropped Cuddy off. People are yelling. Some gather around a man, handing him money while he writes something in a notebook.

"Look!" I nudge Madge. "He's just like you, writing stuff down even in the middle of a ruckus."

"You're kidding, right? He's nothing like me." Madge snorts. "He's taking bets, not trying to get to the bottom of this story."

Her eyes light up. "Want to get closer?" I do not want to get closer. I'm pretty sure the hair on the back of my neck is standing straight up, the air feels so charged, but how can I say no? Only a yellow-bellied mama's boy would do such a thing. So I follow Mad Madge as she dodges under arms and past elbows and swearwords. Because of the fight going on, no one notices two less-than-tall people snaking through the crowd.

I shimmy up to the front, Madge right behind me, and immediately feel like I can't swallow.

Two men. Scrapping and clawing like cats fighting over a dead fish.

And one of them is my dad.

CHAPTER 26

L et's go, Stan," Madge says. She shoves her notebook into her pocket and takes my hand. But she is a lousy leader, because as soon as we break away from the crowd, she leads me right straight into a solid brick wall of a man.

The man lifts my chin.

"Ready to head home?" Stinky Pete asks. Madge pats my arm, then pulls out her notebook before diving back into the throng of people.

I nod to Stinky Pete. He slings his arm around me and guides me down the street.

"Were you dropping Cuddy off?" Stinky Pete asks. His voice is light, but his words seem serious.

I nod again.

"And what is Cuddy up to?" Stinky Pete asks.

I shrug. I can still hear yelling, pulling me back and pushing me away at the same time.

What was my dad doing? Why was he fighting? Will he be okay?

"Your dad will be okay, Stan," Stinky Pete says as we turn toward the boardinghouse. Then he stops. He stops walking. He stops talking. He doesn't even tell me how he knows my dad will be okay.

Instead, he can't seem to find any words. And I immediately see why, because when I look up the street I lose all my words, too. Here comes Mr. Archibald Crutchley, trotting off in his new carriage, tipping his hat as he passes us. And next to him, in her nicest dress and fanciest hat, is my mother. She looks the other way as they go by.

Stinky Pete's eyes follow them as they move in the opposite direction. He sighs. "Some days, Stan, I wonder if it's all worth it," he says.

Once we step in the door, we're immediately met with Granny's cheery whistle and a smirk from Geri, who looks like she's eaten the last piece of pie.

"Well, yes, I did in fact eat the last piece of Granny's pie," Geri says. She licks her lips.

I feel like punching her.

Oh, no. I don't really want to punch her. Or do I? Is it in my blood to want to punch people? Did I get that from my dad? The punching part?

"Probably," Geri answers. It's spooky how she can read my thoughts.

"Only the thoughts that come straight out of your mouth," Geri replies. She's reading another medical book. A new one, it looks like.

"That's quite observant!" Geri says. "Especially for you! Yes, yes, it is a new medical book. It has all the latest diseases and cures. I'll probably be able to cure your dropsy, but it might be too late." She gnaws on the end of her pencil thoughtfully.

I don't have dropsy. I know I don't have dropsy. I'm absolutely 100 percent sure I don't have dropsy. I look toward Stinky Pete; I can trust him to tell me I don't have dropsy, but he left the room. I hear him mumbling to Granny in the kitchen.

Then I remember how I dropped my satchel the other day on the way to school. And I dropped the salt during dinner. The saltshaker didn't break, but it did spill. I tried to throw some salt over my shoulder, but Granny said that was a ridiculous superstition; also, there was enough salt all over the floor and maybe I could just clean that up. And then I said that was a woman's job, and then she said it was also a woman's job to swat the behinds of poorly behaved children, which I would soon learn if I didn't get up and get sweeping lickety-split.

I wasn't scared at all by her big talk, but I did think it was a good idea to clean up the salt, just in case.

Stinky Pete helped me.

And yesterday I dropped my slate during arithmetic and it shattered all over the floor. Miss Wenzel said Marshall, her pet, would never have done such a thing and why can't I be more like Marshall?

I can't be more like Marshall. It's not in my nature to be more like namby-pamby Marshall. Because apparently I come from a long line of fighters.

And obviously I am dying from dropsy.

"Can you come up with a cure soon?" I'm desperate. "Because I've got things to do," I add.

"It was thought that blood-letting or leeching or lancing would help," Geri says, her nose still in her book. "And I've always wanted to try one of those."

"But that's not the case now, right? Right?" I'm worried. There's no one in the world who would like to stab me with a knife, cut me with a lance, or stick leeches on me more than Geri.

She pauses. It's a really

long pause. Evil thoughts apparently take a long time to wind their way through her brain. "No," she finally says.

"So what will we do? I can't keep dropping things! I won't have anything left to drop. It will all be broken!"

"You don't have dropsy," Granny says, thrusting a plate of food in my face. Stinky Pete walks by with his own plate, heading straight for his room without a glance.

I wonder if he'll be down for our nightly game of gin rummy. Or to read the next chapter of *Treasure Island*.

"I'll be down," he says. Then he slowly clunks up the stairs.

Granny peers at me, her arms crossed. "Don't start with your hypochondria again, young man. You're as healthy as a horse, and we have too many actual worries to get wrapped up in imaginary ones," she says, wiping baked beans off my face with her apron. "And don't get food on the sofa," she adds as she heads to the kitchen.

"Did you hear that, Geri? Huh? You should stop making Granny and Mama worry." I point at her with my fork. It bobbles in my hand and I barely catch it before it falls to the floor.

I'm still not sure I don't have dropsy.

Geri laughs. "I'm not the one causing all the worry, Stan," she says, getting up from the sofa.

"What do you mean?" I ask through a mouthful of bread. She's the one who worried everyone by getting sick. She's the one worrying everyone now by telling me I'm sick and am going to die.

"Ha!" Geri snorts. "You're the only one worried you're going to die. Granny and your mother aren't worried about me. They're worried about you."

"What do you mean?" I ask through a mouthful of potato.

"I'm not the one gallivanting around with my ne'er-do-well so-called father, am I?"

"What do you mean?" I ask though a mouthful of beans.

"Or the one neglecting his responsibilities for Cuddy," she adds, scooping up her books.

"What do you mean?" I ask through a mouthful of pork.

"Or the one who has all the adults pulling their hair out with worry that you'll run off or forget to take care of Cuddy or not go to school. You are practically Mr. McLachlan's second job. And your mother is beside herself that you're going to turn into a juvenile delinquent," she says.

"What do you mean?" I ask through a mouthful of milk. Some of which may have landed on the rug.

But Geri is already shutting the door to her room. She opens it a crack and peers out like she's forgotten something important.

"You're the reason your mama's out with Mr. Crutchley tonight, you know."

I choke a little on all the food in my mouth. How? What have I done to cause Mama to take up with Mr. Crutchley? I've done everything to *avoid* that situation.

"Your mother is so worried about your recent behavior, she's pretty sure the best recourse is to send you to boarding school. And the only way that's going to happen is if she marries Mr. Crutchley," Geri says. "Also, you have terrible manners," she adds, then slams the door.

I can't believe she said that. I wipe up the baked beans that have landed on my sock.

My manners are impeccable.

WIDE AWAKE CLUB.

LINCOLN.
HONEST OLD ABE.
The People's Choice.

There are some really good members in this club, but I still wouldn't recommend joining.

CHAPTER 27

I am too young to be burdened with insomnia, the no-good trickster that steals sleep and replaces it with a brain that won't shut off.

I wonder if Geri has a cure for that. And if it's even worth asking.

Oh, who am I kidding. Geri's cure would be worse than the illness. She'd probably knock me out with a hammer and then send me a bill.

Blood thumps in my ears, and thoughts swirl in my brain. Thoughts about my dad and my future and maybe a recipe for snake oil that includes a dead rat and tobacco juice.

I need to write that one down before I forget.

Then I think about my dad again. It's plain as the big nose on Granny's face that my dad is an important man; people take him seriously, and by "seriously" I mean they might be afraid of him. But that's not necessarily a bad thing, right? That's just a sign of respect. Like when people are afraid of the police. Or their teachers. Or grandmothers. He's a man who means business.

It's also clear my dad likes having me around. Otherwise why would he ask me to run his errands? Why would he ask me to stop by?

And why *shouldn't* I spend time with my dad?

But that might no longer be possible now that I'm going to be sent to a boarding school, and if that's the case, I might never see my dad again.

I just found the guy. I can't lose him already.

I close my eyes and try to get my head to stop speeding along like a runaway horse. Mama rustles in the bed next to me. I don't think she's sleeping, either. Why isn't Mama sleeping? Is her brain spinning, too? Geri seems sure Mama would be better off without me, but I know Mama and can't imagine that's true.

To be perfectly honest, however, if I hadn't run into Mrs. Carlisle, Mrs. Carlisle wouldn't have broken her leg. And if

Mrs. Carlisle hadn't broken her leg, she wouldn't have gotten mad at me. And if Mrs. Carlisle hadn't gotten mad at me, she wouldn't have threatened Mama with her doctor bills. And then Mama wouldn't be doing the Carlisles' laundry every week. For free. On top of everything else she does.

Also, if I weren't here, there would be fewer mouths to feed. Especially if, as Granny says, I'm equal to five mouths.

Although I'm not sure if she means I talk as much as five people or eat that much.

Probably both, knowing her.

Mama didn't get home until it was almost dark. She slid in the door, snuck a sidelong glance at Stinky Pete, who didn't look up from our game, then hunched her shoulders and walked up to our room. Stinky Pete stared at her back as she climbed the stairs, his mouth twisted and his eyes worried.

I have no idea what is going on; they're both acting like they've got something to say but they've forgotten how to speak.

I have never had that problem. I'm going to have to check with Geri and see if some kind of ailment is going around.

Also, is it really my fault Mama was out with Mr. Crutchley? She can't be so desperate she would give up all her happiness because of me.

But maybe Geri's right and Mama would be happier if I weren't here.

And if that's the case, why am I staying when I could be with my dad, someone who actually does seem to want me around?

I grab my scrapbook and *Treasure Island* from the bedside table, throw on my trousers, and sneak toward the door.

"Stan?" Mama says, her voice thick with sleep.

"I'll be right back, Mama," I say. She rolls over, the bed-springs letting out a creaky moan as she settles back under the covers.

I tiptoe down the stairs, nab my coat, and jam everything else into my bag.

I stand on the stoop, looking at the merchandise dock. My insides churn the same way they do when I fling myself into the lake for the first time each year. I'm about to make something happen. I could be a well-known Great Lakes captain or a fearsome outlaw or a heartless fighter. Or a cowboy or an explorer or a rich gold miner.

It doesn't matter as long as I'm not Archibald Crutchley's stepson. Or some chicken-livered whippersnapper.

I take a step and a deep breath and turn onto State Street. I steal a glance at the boardinghouse. The kerosene lamp in Stinky Pete's room flickers, and did I see the curtain move?

Oh, what does it matter? I've just taken the first step toward my future. And I am leaving the rest—Geri and her deadly diseases, Cuddy and his never-ending questions, Mad Madge and her never-ending questions, Granny and her bossy ways, Archibald Crutchley and his tippy-toe self, Stinky Pete and . . . and . . . his quotes? His twinkly eyes? His pats on my back? Mama and her warm hugs? The extra bacon she always sneaks on my plate when Granny isn't looking? The way she laughs when I tell her a joke?

I sniff and wipe my eyes. This is not the time to get senti-mental. No, real men don't worry about the past. Not when the future promises to be so exciting.

I think about the last time I saw my dad, how happy he was to see me and how long it's taken me to find him.

I can't stop now because I might not get another chance.

CHAPTER 28

I trudge down the street, kicking a rock, my bag heavy, my feet sluggish. My eyes must be tired because they seem to be a bit watery. And maybe my heart feels heavy, like there's a stone in my chest.

But I perk up as I near the merchandise dock, because how can I not? There's my dad! Meandering out of the State Street Saloon, even though it's really late. Really, really late. And maybe he's not meandering so much as staggering.

He sees me, I think. His head bobbles back and forth in my direction like a chicken or binoculars trying to focus.

"Sthtan!" he slurs. His left eye looks swollen and there's a red gash on his cheek—a reminder of the fight I was trying to forget.

"Ha!" he laughs. "You shud see the udder guy! Hic!" He lays a heavy hand on my arm, steadying himself. I stumble.

"Haf you bin drinkin', son?" he asks. "C'mon. Leth head to the boat. Gotta get my forty winks 'fore we lif the ol' anchor, eh?" He tries to slap my back but sways off balance. I grab him so he doesn't fall.

Oh But You Ought to See The Other Fellow!

I think I'd rather not.

Compliments of *Shaffer* Photographer,
NO. 275 MAIN STREET,   POUGHKEEPSIE, N. Y.

What am I doing? I'm not sure I like this version of my dad. I'm not sure Geri isn't right about him, and I never, ever want to admit to that, so I keep hold of my dad's elbow.

"Wha wud I do wifout you, Sthtan?" he asks. I feel like I'm worth something to him. And like he might fall if I let go of his elbow.

Also, sometimes you get started down a path and it's just easier to keep going and see where it takes you.

Sometimes it takes you to the cemetery and you end up lost in a bunch of graves until it gets dark and you're sure ghosts are going to come and eat you. That only happened once, and then Mad Madge showed up, and even though she called me a toad-spotted giglet and threatened to leave me there, eventually she led me to the road and I made it home before Geri ate all of Granny's baking powder biscuits.

But this path isn't headed to the cemetery—we're going right to the docks. I adjust my bag, weave my arm under my dad's shoulder, and help him to the *Wanderer*.

We wobble up the gangplank. Jeb waits there, half asleep. He jars awake. "Well, well, what do we have here?" He grins.

"Fine thith man a bed, wouldja?" my dad says to Jeb, pointing at him but past him, like his aim is a bit off.

Jeb looks at me and sighs. "Will, do, Cap'n. Joey, take Cap'n to his room!" he snaps.

Joey scampers over like an eager puppy.

"Over here. What's your name?" Jeb motions for me to follow him.

"Stan. Stanley Slater," I say, hoping maybe the last name triggers something in Jeb's brain. "I'm Captain Slater's son," I add. I don't really have much faith in Jeb's brain.

"Ah! Another one of them, eh?" he says. I have no idea what he means, so I simply nod. "You can sleep in here." He thrusts open a door and hooks his lantern inside. The room is about the size of a closet in the boardinghouse, with a bunk and a table and that's about it. Something scurries under the floorboards.

"We're leaving port in about an hour," Jeb says. He squints his eyes and tilts his head. "You sure you want to do this? Sure you're up for a life on the lakes?"

I swallow and nod.

"You sure?" he repeats. "This is not a life for mama's boys," he adds. Is he accusing me of being a mama's boy?

"I was made for a life on the lakes," I say. The boat lurches and I fall on the bunk, my pack still attached, my arms and legs thrown up in the air like an upside-down turtle.

Jeb snickers. "Obviously," he says as I struggle to get upright. "Suit yourself, but we won't be back to these parts for a while," he warns, and shuts the door. The lantern shakes, sending light quivering along the walls.

I slide out of my pack, sit upright, and take a deep breath. This is a really small room. I feel like I'm in a broom closet. There's a broom in the corner.

I am living in a broom closet.

It also smells like the wet socks I forgot under my bed for three weeks.

My socks didn't smell that bad.

SKUNK. Okay, maybe they did.

It's not what I would call a good smell. But I might as well get used to it.

I lie down and look at the wooden slatted ceiling. I am now a sailor. I think this is the closest I've come so far to being a man.

Apparently being a man means you don't always have to be clean—you don't have to bathe, you can fight and swear and stomp in mud puddles and never wash your hair. You should also have a tattoo.

I dig down deep in my bag and pull out my pen. I push up my sleeve past my elbow, baring the top of my arm, and draw a heart. I write MOM in the middle.

There's a small mirror on the wall above the table. I get up to admire my handiwork. Maybe I can become the ship's tattoo artist!

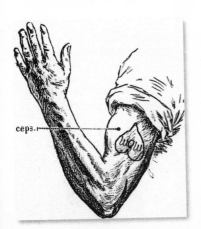

Maybe not. Apparently it's not as easy as I thought to draw on your own arm. I drew a nice heart, but when I wrote MOM, I wrote it upside down. My tattoo might say WOW.

I quickly pull down my sleeve.

I miss Mama. Just a tiny bit. A manly, tiny bit. Not like I'm a mama's boy or anything.

I try not to breathe in very deeply, to avoid the smell, and I close my eyes. I'll need a good night's sleep for the journey ahead, a journey that is going to completely change my entire life.

Every morning Stinky Pete comes into the kitchen whistling. "It's a new day!" he says. "Full of possibilities, Stan!" Like something great could happen at any moment.

If I can go to sleep, before I know it, it will be a new day. And something great could happen tomorrow.

But just as my thoughts start slowly swirling, I'm startled by thumps. And shouts. I jump off my bed, almost hitting my head on the ceiling, and crack open the door.

It's my dad. He obviously has not slept off whatever it was he was supposed to sleep off. He leans against the side of the ship, hurling words to a group of men on the dock.

"Come up here and thay that!" he yells. Jeb holds him back so he doesn't fall off the boat, he's leaning so far over the edge.

I count seven lanterns and maybe more men.

"You can't break a man's leg and then walk off like nothing happened!" one of them yells. The others murmur their agreement, but three men stand near the gangplank, lantern light flicking off the knives in their hands.

"Shur, I can. In fack, I did!" my dad yells, his arm pointing randomly in the air.

"This isn't over, Slater," another man yells. "We want

you and your crew gone. You have thirty minutes before the police get here!" Their footsteps fade as they head down the dock toward town.

Two of the men haul my dad back toward his bunk. He curses and stumbles the whole way.

"Trewley! Larch! Carmine!" Jeb yells to the crew. "Time to go! Let's get the supplies loaded!" He keeps barking orders as I shuffle back to my closet.

My dad doesn't feel safe. Let's face it. He's a criminal, and his crew isn't any better.

But I feel trapped, like it's too late now.

I lie on my bunk, but who am I kidding. I'm not going to sleep anytime soon.

I give up, open my bag, and pull out my scrapbook. Immediately something feels wrong.

I search the pages, my heart thump-thumping. Most of them are blank. What happened to my scrapbook? Did Geri get a hold of it again?

The first picture I flip to is one of Abraham Lincoln. I'm surprised to see my name written on it in Cuddy's handwriting.

Hero? Cuddy thinks I'm a hero? He *has* been listening to me!

Next to the picture of Lincoln is an ad for insurance. Which is a little worrisome.

Get for Stan!
Because he always gets in accidents!

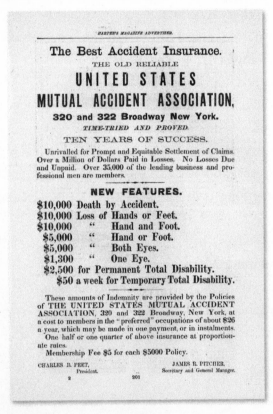

He could make a lot of money if he died. Or lost his hands.

I turn the page. It's filled with ads for food. And my name again. My stomach grumbles just reading it.

Get Stan all the food.
He's always hungry.

Stan needs to eat a lot.
He's strong.
And brave.
And that makes people hungry.

Why didn't I grab some bacon before I left the house?

Pictures of derring-do cover the next page. And my name is on all of them. According to Cuddy, I can climb mountains.

Save people from burning buildings.

Or he might think I'm a dog. You never know with Cuddy.

Best of all, he thinks I'm funny.

Obviously my sense of humor has been rubbing off on him.

FRANCIS WILSON AS HOOLAH GOOLAH IN THE "OOLAH."
Drawn by A. E. Sterner, after a photograph by Sarony.—From the collection of Evert Jansen Wendell.

I'm holding Cuddy's scrapbook. It looks exactly like mine, except I am much better at the art of scrapbooking. I do like his subject matter, however. And how much he appreciates my many talents.

Except I'm not all too sure I've been living up to what he

thinks of me. And it might be too late. I hear the men out on the deck shouting, getting the boat ready to leave St. Ignace. And who knows when it will return.

I stuff Cuddy's scrapbook in my satchel and open my door just as some of the crew jog down the dock, untying ropes and yelling at each other.

"Get inside!" one growls. But I have to get out of here. I have to get off this boat, run home, climb into bed, and pretend this has never happened.

Tomorrow is a new day. Tomorrow I'll be a new fellow.

I try to dodge one of the men, but Jeb grabs my arm. "In your cabin, kid. Cap'n's son or not, we'll run you into the floor if we have to."

"I need to get off," I say. "I . . . I've got things to do. I've got school in the morning!"

Jeb scoffs. "All you really need to do is get outta the way." His grip tightens as he pulls me toward my smelly broom closet of a room.

"Be happy you've got that," Jeb says, opening the door.

"He said he wants to get off the boat," a voice says from the shadows of the dock.

Jeb looks around, peering into the dark. "Yeah, well, what are *you* going to do about it?" His fingers dig into my arm.

I wonder that, too. The guys are beginning to haul the gangplank up into the boat, and there's no turning around after that. After we set sail, I'm done for. My life as a law-abiding citizen is over, and I'll probably be on the run from the sheriff for the rest of my livelong days.

Suddenly the boat shifts and I almost lose my balance. It's Stinky Pete! He has one boot on the gangplank, one hand on a sailor's collar, and the other hand on the ropes attached to the ramp. He lifts the sailor and dangles him over the water. The guy squirms more than Miss Wenzel's favorite student, Marshall Curtis, slipping on a patch of ice.

I didn't push him. Honest.

"You want me to drop you?" Stinky Pete asks the sailor. "Because I have no problem doing that." He makes like he's going to let go, and the fellow immediately stops moving. Stinky Pete focuses on Jeb. "Let the young man off the boat," he says calmly.

Jeb lets go of me but takes a step toward Stinky Pete. "Don't think I will," he says. "Don't think his father, the cap'n, would 'preciate that." I'm not sure it matters to me what my dad would or wouldn't appreciate. Not now that I might be stuck with him forever. "And I don't 'preciate other people telling me what or what not to do," Jeb adds.

"I don't really care what you or what that sorry excuse for a man would or wouldn't appreciate," Stinky Pete says. He walks up the gangplank, still dragging the sailor by the collar. Jeb swallows, his Adam's apple quivering. "Let's ask Stan what he wants, shall we?"

I try to slide around Jeb but he juts out his arm to stop me. "You're not going anywhere," he says, never taking his eyes off Stinky Pete. Three men stand to the side, their fists clenched, knives glinting in the dim lantern light.

Stinky Pete takes a quick glance around and shoves one of the guys aside, forcing the other two to fall to the deck. They don't seem like they're in much of a rush to get up. He stomps onto the boat, still dragging the first sailor.

"Stan," Stinky Pete asks, "what would *you* like?"

And I realize this is one of the 115 reasons I love this guy. No one ever asks me what I would like except him.

The other 114 reasons mainly have to do with reading together in the evening, playing cards with him on the front porch, laughing about something Granny said while we eat her pie, and just the fact that he likes me.

"I want to go home," I say. "With you."

Stinky Pete smiles. "There's your answer, man," he says to Jeb. Then he takes the sailor he'd been holding all this time and thrusts him hard at Jeb. Both men fall down. There's all sorts of fumbling and rustling and men jostling all over the deck.

We turn toward home, a heaviness in my chest. What if I never see my dad again? Mama always says there's a little bit of good in everyone, and I've been waiting to see that part in my dad.

A door slams open, making both Stinky Pete and me jolt midstep on the gangplank.

"Shtop! Lishen here, whoever you shink you are!" It's my dad, weaving his way toward us. "Heesh comin' wish me!" But he only gets a couple of steps through the door before he heaves his head over the side, losing his dinner in the process.

My dad, who was supposed to be my hero, isn't who I imagined he would be. I like my imaginary version a whole lot better.

"You can't choose your relatives, son," Stinky Pete says, staring at my dad. "But you can choose your family." He takes my hand and looks at me. "You know I wasn't going to leave you here, right? I can't be the only man at that boarding-house, now, can I?" he adds, smiling.

I smile in return. What was I thinking? Captain Arthur Slater, hero of the seas, may be my father, but Stinky Pete makes a much better dad.

Also, I can't leave him alone at that boardinghouse with all those bossy women. That would be like leaving a baby with a pack of hungry wolves.

Stinky Pete chuckles. "Only worse, right?" He pulls me into a hug. "Thanks for looking out for me," he says.

I nod. Someone has to.

CHAPTER 29

"I was so tired last night, I don't think I moved at all," Mama says. Stinky Pete raises his eyebrows at me over his coffee. "I did have some odd dreams, however," she adds.

Stinky Pete winks. "Yeah?" he asks. "What about?"

Mama sits down, leans her head on her hands, and looks at him. "You." Stinky Pete chokes, his cheeks reddening. "And Stan," she adds, kissing the top of my head before getting up.

I look at Stinky Pete. Does she know? Am I in trouble?

"You're always in trouble," Geri says. I didn't think she was listening since her nose is buried in another medical book.

"I'm always listening," she says, her eyes barely peeping over the cover.

"What was your dream about?" I ask.

Mama smiles, looking down at the oatmeal she's stirring. "Let's just say I like the two of you together." This time her cheeks flush.

Stinky Pete's grin is so big it swallows half his face.

"Alice," Granny says, bustling in, "Archibald will be here in a half hour. Don't you think you should make yourself presentable?" She straightens the salt and pepper shakers on the table before grabbing an apron.

Stinky Pete falls into himself like a collapsible chair at the mention of Mr. Crutchley. But Mama doesn't even turn around and barely acknowledges Granny.

"He won't be coming over, Mother."

Granny stops midtie of her apron. "What—what do you mean?" she splutters.

"I mean, he won't be coming over," Mama says. She adds salt to the pan and continues stirring.

Does this mean what I think it means?

"But—but . . . ," Granny stammers. "But what about money for the house? What about Stan's education? His juvenile delinquency?" Her voice sounds like the hum of a teakettle right before it boils. "What about removing him from the influence of his father?"

Stinky Pete suddenly perks up. "I don't think that's going to be a problem, right, Stan?" he says, nudging me. Honestly, I don't know if he's more excited about Mr. Crutchley no longer being around or my dad leaving.

"Both," Geri says. "But we're all glad the *Wanderer* was nowhere to be seen this fine morning. Frankly, I was getting tired of babysitting you."

"How do you know it's gone? You haven't even left the house," I ask. I choose to ignore the babysitting remark, it's so ridiculous. Sometimes being a man means ignoring women.

"Oh, I would not recommend that if I were you," Geri warns. "Women don't like being ignored." She licks her finger and turns the page of her book, and a chill runs up my spine. "Many a man has died from ignoring a woman," she says.

I clear my throat and quickly change the subject. "But how do you know my da—the *Wanderer* is gone?"

"I went to the store to get some milk and ran into Madge." She shakes her head in admiration. "That girl knows what's going on, that's for sure. A woman after my own heart."

Mama sets a plate of eggs and bacon and toast in front of Stinky Pete. He beams at her like she's saved his life.

"So," Granny says, looking at Stinky Pete and Mama as if there's some invisible thread between them and she can't quite decide how to cut it. "How on earth do you plan on paying for this place?" She snorts.

"We've got it figured out, right, Peter?" Mama says. Her eyes don't leave Stinky Pete's. He just nods a goofy, happy nod.

He has the same look on his face as Cuddy when he's talking to Geri.

Oh, my good Lord above. Stinky Pete and Mama are in love.

Geri throws her book down and her hands in the air. "You can't be serious, Stan." She leans toward me and peers into my eyes. It's uncomfortable.

She simply can't handle it when I know something and she doesn't.

"Stan, your mother and Mr. McLachlan have been courting for the last three months," she says, planting her hands on the table before standing up.

"Wh-what about when she went on that ride with Mr. Crutchley?" I stammer.

"Oh, that." Geri waves a hand. "You had your mother all in a panic. She lost her senses for a minute."

Mama nods sheepishly. "I did," she says. "I'm sorry, Peter." He takes both of her hands in his.

Geri points back and forth between Mama and Stinky Pete like she's tapping out a message on a typewriter.

"Will you two just make it official already?" Geri asks. "It's obvious you like

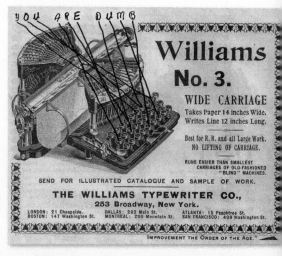

each other. Just get it over with. Then at least Stan can stop obsessing about whether or not Mr. Crutchley is going to be his stepfather."

Stinky Pete grins at Mama. Then he does something completely unexpected.

He falls onto one knee. Right there in the middle of the kitchen.

Is he okay? Is Stinky Pete okay?

I move to help the guy back on his feet when Geri grabs my arm. I am the only one concerned for Stinky Pete's health, apparently. So much for the doctor, here.

"Don't you do a thing," Geri says through her teeth. "He's going to ask her to marry him."

What? People actually do that?

"Alice Nelson Slater"—he clears his throat—"will you make me the happiest man in the world and accept my hand in marriage?" Stinky Pete asks. He's got one of Mama's hands in his, and he's shaking like a dry autumn leaf.

Mama doesn't move. She stands with a wooden spoon in her hand like she's ready to knight Stinky Pete.

I hold my breath. What if she says no? She can't say no! But what if she does?

Don't say no. Don't say no.

Mama drops the spoon, pulls Stinky Pete to his feet, and throws her arms around him.

I'm pretty sure that's a yes. I clap. I'm so happy, I clap and clap and maybe hoot and holler.

Geri claps, too. Even Granny, leaning against the kitchen

sink, has a hand over her mouth, hiding a smile. A smile so big she can't even hide it.

I don't know if I've ever seen Granny smile before. Her face is probably cracking and that's why she has to hide it behind her hand.

Stinky Pete pulls me into a giant bear hug, big enough to hold me and Mama. Then Geri. And even Granny joins in.

I peek at her face. It's wrinkly, but surprisingly it didn't crack.

I don't know who thinks these things are cute.

Boo-hoo! Pa's going to the Union Clothing Company's Excursion and won't take me.

Poor Cuddy

CHAPTER 30

The last day of school is my favorite. I was looking forward to hanging out with Stinky Pete, but then he reminded me that he has a job. So I was looking forward to hanging out with Eugene "Genius" Malone, but then he reminded me that he now has a job maintaining the Methodist Episcopal Church. So I was looking forward to sitting on the front porch eating bacon all summer, but then Granny reminded me that I have a job, too.

Mrs. Law asked if I could continue watching Cuddy over the summer. His mother is a bit under the weather.

"She's going to have a baby, Stan," Cuddy whispers.

"But we're not supposed to talk about it in front of anyone."

Of course not! Who cares about babies?

"I love babies," Madge says from across the room. My
respect for her as a bully just dropped to zero. "They always
smell so good and are so little and helpless." She and Geri
are working on a plan to form some sort of venomous group
at school in the fall.

"Feminist, Stan," Geri says. "We simply want men and
women to be treated equally."

I roll my eyes and smile at Cuddy. "Women," I say, shaking my head.

But Cuddy just looks at me, scissors in his hand. "They're
right, Stan," he says. We're sitting on the sofa, going through
Granny's old magazines.

At least I hope they're the old ones. If not, I'll just blame
it on Cuddy.

Cuddy still stares at me. "Grandmother says we're way
behind the times." He's as serious as a case of measles when
he says it.

"Do you think I have measles?" Cuddy asks. His hand
darts to his face, and I grab the scissors he's holding before
he stabs himself.

"You don't have measles, Cuddy," Geri says. It's the first
time I've heard her actually *not* try to kill someone with a
diagnosis, but she does have a soft spot for Cuddy.

"You're so lucky you have a doctor in the family, Stan,"
Cuddy says, gazing at Geri.

"Bad luck, you mean," I mumble. "Do you want me to help you cut out some pictures, Cud?" I offer. Because I am whiz with scissors, I don't mind saying.

I also have a plan.

After I cut out the picture, I paste it smack-dab in the middle of the page before writing on it.

I may not know what it takes to be a cowboy or gold miner. I may never get rich quick. I may eat too much bacon, and I may not have the best manners.

But I am a whiz at being a friend, I don't mind saying.

AUTHOR'S NOTE

A lot of research goes into writing a historical novel. Much of what I learned isn't even included in the book, but it was important to know Stan's world since it was so much different from ours. I researched not-very-exciting topics like plumbing (indoor toilets? outhouses? chamber pots?) and what streets looked like (paved? gravel? mud?). I also researched more interesting things like the giant squid, snake oil, and the 1893 Chicago World's Fair, and because I'm a kind person (not to mention smart and witty), I'm going to share those sources with *you*!

NINETEENTH-CENTURY MEDICINE

Without the Internet, it wasn't as easy for information to be transmitted in the 1800s, which meant it took time for people to learn about advances in medicine. In Stan's world, the theory that germs caused illnesses was relatively new, hospitals were not common, women doctors (as Stan could tell you) were rare, and "cures" might contain anything from ammonia to opium.

Curious about how medicine has changed through the years? This timeline of medical advances covers everything from Hippocrates to the present:

"Medical Advancements Timeline," Information Please Database. infoplease.com/ipa/A0932661.html

Although my own mother made me wash my hands every three minutes, germ theory wasn't why mortality rates decreased in the late nineteenth century. Want to know the reason? Or more about health practices? Check out this resource:

"Germ Theory," Harvard University Library, Open Collections Program. ocp.hul.harvard.edu/contagion/germtheory.html

Be thankful you have access to twenty-first-century medicine rather than what Stan had at his disposal:

"Medical Treatments in the Late 19th Century," The Rose Melnick Medical Museum. melnickmedicalmuseum.com/2013/03/27/19ctreatment

Before the Pure Food and Drug Act of 1906, it was possible for just about anyone to whip up a batch of pretty much anything and call it medicine, which is exactly what our hero, Stan, tries to do. This bogus medicine is called snake oil and has a very interesting history:

"A History of Snake Oil Salesmen," National Public Radio. npr.org /sections/codeswitch/2013/08/26/215761377/a-history-of-snake-oil -salesmen

LIVING IN THE 1890S

When I decided the Carlisles would hire Stan to watch Cuddy, I had to determine how much they would pay him—twenty-five cents today certainly wouldn't go very far, but in 1895 it was worth a lot more. This site helped me figure out what things cost in the late nineteenth century.

Samuel H. Williamson, "Seven Ways to Compute the Relative Value of a U.S. Dollar Amount, 1774 to present," Measuring Worth. measuringworth.com/uscompare

What was life like for Stan and Geri?

Mancini, Mark. "24 Sure Signs You're an 1890s Kid." mentalfloss.com /article/56772/24-sure-signs-youre-1890s-kid

AMAZING WOMEN OF THE NINETEENTH CENTURY

I've mentioned Nellie Bly and Elizabeth Blackwell as heroes in this book, but the nineteenth century included many equally amazing women. It's definitely worth reading more about them!

Susan B. Anthony, suffragette
greatwomen.org/inductee/susan-b-anthony

Elizabeth Blackwell, physician
nlm.nih.gov/exhibition/changingthefaceofmedicine/physicians
/biography_35.html

Nellie Bly, journalist
nellieblyonline.com

Queen Liliuokalani, Hawaii's last monarch
aloha-hawaii.com/hawaii/queen-liliuokalani

Madame C. J. Walker, self-made millionaire
madamewalker.net/History/tabid/537/Default.aspx

TIMBER PIRATES

To be perfectly honest, I didn't even know timber pirates existed until I researched lumbering. I based Stan's father on Roaring Dan Seavey.

Boyd, Dr. Richard J. "Roaring Dan Seavey: The Pirate of Lake Michigan." hsmichigan.org/wp-content/uploads/2012/04/DanSeavey.pdf

Kates, Kristi. "Pirates of the Great Lakes," *Northern Express.* northern-express.com/michigan/article-6127-pirates-of-the-great-lakes.html

Williams, Rebecca. "Sure there were Pirates in the Caribbean, but the Great Lakes had them too." Michigan Radio. michiganradio. org/post/sure-there-were-pirates-caribbean-great-lakes-had-them-too#stream/0

1893 CHICAGO WORLD'S FAIR

From May through October 1893, Chicago played host to the World's Columbian Exposition, a huge fair spanning hundreds of acres and entertaining millions of visitors. Forty-six nations participated, setting up pavilions that contained everything from German artillery to a Viking ship. The Ferris wheel was introduced, along with Juicy Fruit gum, and an entire exhibit was dedicated to electricity. It was also the backdrop for murder—the mayor was shot and killed two days before the end of the fair. And that's just a sampling of what went on during the exposition.

Maranzani, Barbara, "7 Things You May Not Know About the 1893 Chicago World's Fair," History in the Headlines, *History*. history.com/news/7-things-you-may-not-know-about-the-1893-chicago-worlds-fair

World's Columbian Exposition, Chicago Historical Society. chicagohs.org/history/expo.html

Opening the Vaults: Wonders of the 1893 World's Fair, The Field Museum. worldsfair.fieldmuseum.org

THE GIANT SQUID

Once thought to be mermen or sea monks, photographs had been taken proving the existence of giant squids by the time Cuddy's uncle saw one in Newfoundland. Because they're so elusive, however, we still don't know much about them, which makes them all the more fascinating.

"Giant squid: What do you know about these weird and mysterious creatures?" Natural History Museum, London. nhm.ac.uk/kids-only/life/life-sea/giant-squid

Robey, Jason, "Top 10 Startling Giant Squid Facts," InsideDiscovery. blogs.discovery.com/show-news/2013/01/top-10-startling-giant-squid-facts.html

Roper, Clyde, et al., "Giant Squid," Ocean Portal, Smithsonian National Museum of Natural History. ocean.si.edu/giant-squid

OPTICAL ILLUSIONS

When we view optical illusions, our brains are tricked into seeing something that isn't actually there. Often confusing, sometimes unbelievable, and almost always lots of fun, optical illusions teach us about how our brains work.

"Lots and Lots and Lots of Illusions," National Institute of Environmental Health Science. kids.niehs.nih.gov/games/illusions/lots_of _illusions.htm

Orwig, Jessica, "10 mind-melting optical illusions that will make you question reality," *Business Insider.* sciencealert.com/10-mind-melting -optical-illusions-that-will-make-you-question-reality

And here are some optical illusions from the 1800s:
Livewire Puzzles. puzzles.ca/optical_illusions.html

The best part about research is stumbling upon things you don't know and want to know more about. For even more information about research, writing, and Stan, visit my website, alisondecamp.com.

IMAGE CREDITS

Alice (my mother's mother)

Somehow I won the jackpot in the awesome grandmothers contest, which is a contest that doesn't actually exist, but I feel like I've won it anyway.

It's not a coincidence that Stan's mother's is named Alice. Just like Alice in the book, my grandmother Alice married at the ripe old age of fifteen and had my uncle Stan a year later. And then she was basically on her own to raise him. She did an incredible job, even making sure he attended Michigan Agricultural College (now known as Michigan State University), where he graduated with a degree in engineering. By this time Alice had married my grandfather and had my mother, Joan.

Even though Alice had very little education herself, attending college was nonnegotiable for both her son *and* daughter. Alice's thinking was if you educate the man, you educate the man, but if you educate the woman, you educate the family. Alice also wanted her daughter to be able to support herself if need be. She was a feminist way ahead of her time.

Marie (my father's mother)

My grandmother Marie also valued an education. After high school, she approached her father about attending secretarial school, and he said absolutely not—women should be in the home, not in the workforce. Fortunately, Marie didn't listen. Instead, she worked and sent herself to school in Ypsilanti, Michigan. After graduation she answered an ad for a secretarial job in South America. On her way to board the ship, she stopped in Florida and ended up staying there, eventually meeting my grandfather Otto.

Marie never stopped working; she wasn't content staying at home, and rather than marrying someone like her father, she chose a man who valued her strength and intelligence. This was a woman who drove herself to the hospital when it was time to deliver her first baby, and loved reading so much that she spent precious money on the Book-of-the-Month Club.

I see a lot of these women in Geri and Mad Madge, and it's what I love about them—women who won't take no for an answer. I also love Stan's begrudging admiration for the women in his life—whether he quite realizes it or not, he'd be lost without them. These are women who ignore insecure men who are too small-minded to see their worth. My grandmothers' example is the reason my sister and I always believed we could do anything and be anything. It's why I'm a writer and my sister is a world-renowned expert in milk quality (it's a real thing!). It's why my brother married another strong woman. And it's why you, whether you're a boy or a girl, should believe you can do anything and be anything, too.